I AM ZOË HANDKE

I AM ZOË HANDKE

A novel by Eric Larsen

ALGONQUIN BOOKS OF CHAPEL HILL

1992

Published by
Algonquin Books of Chapel Hill
Post Office Box 2225
Chapel Hill, North Carolina 27515–2225
a division of
Workman Publishing Company, Inc.
708 Broadway
New York, New York 10003

Grateful acknowledgment is made to the following publications, in which
sections of this book first appeared: *The Ohio Review* (a portion of Part V,
in somewhat changed form, under the title "Zoë's Dream: August 1977");
and *The New England Review and Bread Loaf Quarterly* (Part I, under
the title "The Death of Leonora"). Reprinted by permission from *New
England Review*, Vol. VII, No. 1 (Autumn 1984).

Library of Congress Cataloging-in-Publication Data

Larsen, Eric, 1941–
I am Zoë Handke : a novel/by Eric Larsen.
p. cm.
ISBN 0-945575-86-6
I. Title.
PS3562.A732I18   1992
813'.54—dc20   91-29783 CIP

2 4 6 8 10 9 7 5 3

For Anne

For there she was.

—Virginia Woolf, *Mrs. Dalloway*

I

ALMA, ILLINOIS

I

I am taller than my mother, although not very much so, perhaps an inch, certainly not more. But I am larger than she was.
My bones are heavier, somehow more angular, more squared-
off with one another. My flesh is thicker. It seems to me that
all my life, in comparison with my slighter and now vanished
mother, I have been made to feel clumsy.

Even near the end of her life, in spite of the madness and
ill health that finally crippled her, carried her in and out of
institutions, and destroyed her, my mother kept the girlish slen-
derness that brought praise to her when she was young from
those who saw in her a desirable and childlike beauty. Only
in the last handful of years before her death did my mother
decline suddenly into the wasting scrawniness of what in her
case passed for old age. But until that late and delayed time,
her body did not greatly change. Her legs and hips remained

slender and attractive. Her waist was narrow and slim. Her breasts, unlike my own, were small and discreet. Even quite near the end of her life, men sometimes approached her in airports or at the entryways to department stores or restaurants, asking if she were lost or in need of directions. As always, I was embarrassed by her response in such situations—the way she pretended to be helpless and flustered when in fact she was neither—because I knew it to be pretended, calculated, and false. Those who did not know her, however, who saw her for the first time, were just as likely to see her quite differently: as plucky, alert, and vivacious. In the uncertainties of my grief for my dead mother, I wish I knew as little as they.

When I was born, in March of 1941, my mother was nineteen years old. For all my life I have been aware that I gave her great anguish at my birth. Presenting myself to the world sideways (the first part seen of me was a curled hand, which I was forced to withdraw) and then feet first, I resisted birth for sixteen hours, from sundown on March twelfth until midmorning of the next day, as if in a long and confused effort not to leave my mother's young body. In the process of this struggle, I brought us both to exhaustion and, as I have so often heard the story, alarmingly near death.

I think of this event now—almost four decades ago, in a white room with steel tables, midnight blackness pressing up against curtainless windows—as the first occasion of my bringing displeasure to my mother through no will of my own. She was too young—and, I believe now, too troubled—ever to acknowledge entirely that I was without malice or blame in this event. Of course I was innocent, but whether her resentment of me was just or unjust makes little difference. I was born into my mother's madness. I know now that other causes for her anger and unhappiness existed before that long night of pain and fear that resulted, surprisingly, in my birth.

Born into the midst of her own youth, I am frightened often when I think of my closeness in age to my mother. The numbers are capable of astonishing me. When I was five years old and about to start school, my mother was a girl of only twenty-four. When I was a decade old, she was not yet thirty. I was a senior in college before my mother at last celebrated her fortieth birthday.

Sometimes I think: *We could have been sisters.* On my mother's rather populous side of the family, I knew sisters whose ages in fact were separated by more than nineteen years—my grandmother's sisters, my mother's aunts. This closeness in age in the case of myself and my mother—even now, when I have lived to the age of forty and have children of my own—is able to confuse and alarm me. Especially recently, it holds for me at certain moments an uprushing of fear and panic that I have spoken of to no one and that draws me unwillingly toward the stopped time that I think of as the past.

My mother, in keeping with the style of the 1940s, covered her mouth generously with vivid red lipstick. Her dark hair, pinned back from her ears, fell to her shoulders and ended there in a loose upturn of curls that seemed to me a perfection of carefully planned disorder. On her cheeks she wore a rouge of light rose, a color taken, it seems to me now, from summertime in the country, where beaded dew lay early in the morning on clustered flowers in sunlit gardens. Sitting on the edge of the bed near my mother's dressing table, I watched her apply this rouge, touching it first to her cheek with the pads of two fingers, then moving them in slowly expanding circles over her skin until it seemed that the blood had rushed there permanently in a rosy blush of healthfulness, or of confusion, or desire.

Perhaps I was four years old at this time, perhaps slightly older. Quietly, careful to be no disturbance, I watched my mother at her mirror. With taps of a soft puff, she touched powder to her white forehead. She pressed her fingers tightly against her temples and with painful attentiveness scrutinized for long moments her image in the glass. She stood up from her chair, placed her hands at her waist, and, her eyes still seeking out the mirror, twirled around until her skirt flared out, rose up, and billowed on the air.

An uncle came to visit at our house. He was what I think of now as one of my numerous questionable uncles—a relative of distant and uncertain connection to my family, and a man as well of uncertain character. Within a decade his marriage was to fail, the blame to be placed on alcohol, and his death was to occur—as it was to occur, too, with other relatives of my family—when he had reached only his middle forties, a time by which, testament to his troubled life, he was to have been variously unemployed, hospitalized, and imprisoned.

He came to our house on a hot summer morning in 1946, having traveled by car from Denver, Colorado. I was five years old. I remember that the white lace curtains in our living room hung motionlessly in front of windows that were thrown open to the hushed, midmorning air outside. I remember that my uncle seemed to fill up the front doorway with his big frame, that his legs were spread slightly apart, that his face was ruddy and round and that it seemed to be beaming with a kind of greatly expectant jollity. I remember that, standing in the door, he extended his hands toward my mother and said, in words that burst forth from him almost in song:

"Will you look at this? Will you just look at this pretty slip of a girl?"

He took my mother under the arms, raised her up, and, in spite of her shrieks of protest, stepped into the middle of the room and swung her around. It seems to me, although perhaps I am wrong, that he held her over his head as he did so, that his strong arms were raised up high, that my mother skimmed as if weightlessly just beneath the ceiling as she flew around in wide circles over his head, like a young bride floating on air in a painting by Marc Chagall.

Memory can be deceitful. Perhaps my mother did not float softly. Perhaps she did not skim just under the ceiling. Perhaps these things are a child's shaping memory, not truth. But I was there, and, unnoticed for the moment, I stood watching. I know that for a certain time on a summer morning in 1946 my mother was raised up on the muscular arms of my uncle, this robust column of a man with the deep rolling laughter in his throat, a patch of sweat darkening the back of his blue shirt, and, lying wait in his future, misery and failure and death. I know that each time my mother's feet swung toward me, I saw her white legs disappearing up under her flying skirt, and I know that the moment shocked me slightly and placed a light touch of fear at my heart.

2

We lived in Three Islands, Illinois, on a working-class street half a block from the Chicago and Grafton Canal. It seems to me at certain moments now that history has come to nothing, and, when I think back, I am reminded of how much I romanticized the canal.

On summer nights from my bed I would from time to time hear a barge going by: if the night was sufficiently still, I would hear through my window the deep-throated drone of its diesel engines, the steady wash of water at its stern as it passed by. At certain times in my adolescence I envied the bargemen, believing that their lives were enchanted and made significant by the simple fact of their journeying endlessly through the land. Lying in my bed in the darkness, I imagined that I was one of them. I imagined long warm nights moving under the dome of a star-filled sky, and summer days on the Illinois River passing slowly between prairie fields of tall drying grass drenched by sunlight. In my imagination, the smooth breadth of the Mississippi carried me toward the fragrant air of the Deep South, where trees in shawls of hanging moss crowded the shores like mourning women, dark shadows gathering at their ankles near where the smooth black water glided over their feet. Certain names were of great importance to my reverie: Hannibal, Cairo, Sainte Genevieve, Memphis, the beautiful syllables of Helena. Like the places in many of the books I read at this time—books that I read always for their mood, never for their meaning—these places and names seemed to me exotic and alluring. Even the pages of Dickens filled me with desire. *"Ours was the marsh country,"* I read with a silent and secret envy, *"down by the river, within, as the river wound, twenty miles of the sea."*

Locked far inland from the sea, feeling that I lived nowhere, I allowed myself for a certain time to imagine that the canal was my river, that it was my sea. Within reach very nearly of my bedroom window, it was the canal, if that should become necessary, that could carry me away.

But of course it did not. My imaginings were in vain. The canal took me nowhere.

(On a small farm in the southern part of the state, near a crossroads town named Alma, Illinois, lived my mother's younger sister Leonora with her two children and her husband William. I was once a house guest there, in the summer when I was twelve years old, a year before Leonora's sudden and premature death. During that visit—a month of long summer days filled with the gentleness of Leonora, of farmhouse nights that were dark and hushed and still—I thought: *I love Leonora. I wish Leonora were my mother.*

Years later, when I was away from home in college, I was to have a recurring dream of visiting the farm. In this dream, it seemed to me that Leonora was still alive, although in the dream I knew also that she had died. I would see myself lying in my bedroom in my family's house in Three Islands. Then I would be on the canal, lying on my back, floating in a small woven basket. Leonora's farm was two hundred miles away. The canal carried me silently and smoothly under a nighttime sky to the Illinois River, and that river carried me southwestward across the entirety of the state to the night-shadowed breadth of the smooth Mississippi. At a place where Illinois lay on one side of the river and Missouri on the other, I was brought up against the embankment. I knew that if I were to crawl up the steep embankment through the underbrush and thorns, I would find a dust-covered country road; and I knew that three miles down that road lay Leonora's farm.

In the dream, however, I never climbed the embankment or found the road. In the dream, I never arrived at the farm. Repeated many times, it was a dream with no conclusion.)

During the years of World War II, my father worked in the shipyards of Pearl Harbor. With other men who were also far from home he repaired steam turbines and pipe fittings in the bowels of deep-hulled ships that would then labor westward through the heavy waters of the Pacific in search of battle with the Japanese.

In my father's absence, I lived with my mother in the silence and stillness of Three Islands, far inland from the sea, waiting for the war to end. That time was now very long ago, and memory of it comes to me only in glimpses, as if from some small distant room where little happens, where there is only slight movement, and where the air is extremely quiet. I remember that shafts of sunlight, on certain days, came in through the kitchen windows of our house, touching the table and floor. I remember that nested into a corner of my upstairs bedroom stood a dollhouse built by my father, with tiny hinges on the window shutters so that they could be opened and closed. And I remember, on certain mornings after the mail had arrived, my mother reading letters from my father. She sat, at those times, at the kitchen table, and while she read I made my way, in cautious and precarious silence, from room to room of the house, waiting for her to be finished. I did not go into the kitchen. Through the doorway between the kitchen and dining room, as I passed by, I could see her at the table, a cup of coffee nearby, and a glass ashtray that caught the light of the sun, and smoke rising in a thin line from the cigarette she held in her fingers.

By some trick of my child's memory, it seems to me now that in those years of waiting for my father's return there was only one season; the memories I possess seem all to have been compressed into the season of early spring, the gray blustery month of March, or the first chill, sunny weeks of April. I was not yet in school. In the late mornings my mother and I went to the store for groceries through gusty winds under gray skies, breathing into our lungs air that was wet and soft and cold. Our coats flapped out behind us, pushed away from our legs, and, as we walked, we passed small houses crowded closely together in rows, their shallow windows pressing forward against the narrow street. If I raised my glance toward their rooftops, I saw tendrils of coal smoke from brick chimneys rising briefly against the gray sky. Then, in the wind, they would be torn away like bits of soiled rag, vanishing into the damp, turbulent air.

On a day when the sun was shining, my mother lied to me about the canal. I remember the moment with the peculiar, uncluttered vividness that can come from a very great distance in time. It was one of those days in early spring when the frail warmth of the sun, penetrating briefly, is carried away repeatedly by buffets of wind that toss the bare branches of trees.

At the end of our street, where it met the canal, was a narrow grass-covered area that we called the park. I sat there on a slatted wooden bench with my mother, and she told me that she had once seen two children who had drowned in the canal. These children, my mother told me, went undiscovered for a day and a night, their bodies floating face down at a place where weeds and rushes grew thickly along a curve in the bank. When at last they were drawn out of the canal the next morning, their faces were found to have been eaten away by eels, leaving hollow caverns where their cheeks and lips and eyes had been.

I do not, of course, remember her exact words; but I remember clearly the quietly captivating, intimate, story-telling caresses of her voice; and I know that these are the images that remain with me still from what my mother told me on that morning in the spring. Nor, however odd it may seem, do I remember having been frightened. I do remember playing afterward, a little self-consciously, on the matted brown grass of the small park and glancing back periodically toward my mother where she sat on the bench—perhaps to make certain, as if in a fairy tale, that she was still there. And I remember also sitting beside her later and peering closely at her face. What I saw (it is an image as clear to me now as if it were yesterday) was the pretty face of a twenty-four-year-old girl: her eyes were closed contentedly; her head was tipped back so that the sunlight fell evenly across her features; the chill wind touched and moved the curls of her hair where they fell loosely over the upturned collar of her coat.

I suppose, given the vulnerable logic of childhood, that I must have been frightened by the story my mother told me. I suppose that there must have been nights when I lay awake in my bed, terrified that I, too, would be drowned in the canal and have my face eaten away. And yet if those fears existed, they have disappeared from my memory. I have no desire to replace them there, or to imagine them. I am a grown woman. I know quite clearly what I have forgotten.

And yet there is something that I do wonder about. I wonder if, in some child's way, I was struck three and a half decades ago by the same thing that most impresses me now when I look back at that distant moment: by the easeful placidity and calmness, the restful satisfaction, the amazing and animal contentedness of my mother's pretty face in the April sunlight after she had told me the story of the two young children drowned in the water of the canal, their faces eaten away by the sharp teeth of eels.

As I got older, growing into adolescence and early adulthood, I was to become accustomed to my mother's habitual lies, although the time was never to arrive when I would stop being humiliated and grieved by them. The world as it actually existed seemed incapable of satisfying my mother; some greater need drove her, as if it were a part of her nature endlessly to weave fabrications and tales, sometimes macabre, sometimes mundane, often increasingly elaborate and contrived, like the plots of the Gothic and mystery and romance novels from which, I later came to realize, my mother gathered the germs for many of her inventions and embroideries.

When I was in my early years of high school, the story recurred at the dinner table from time to time that my mother had been taken to lunch by the chairman of the board, who praised her skill and poise at the switchboard above those of all the others she worked with. At another time she saw a man struck by a taxi on Michigan Avenue who, when she rushed to him, clung to her with such fear and need that she rode with him in the ambulance and, with the doctors' special permission, held the patient's hand through surgery and until the moment of his death. My mother won the half-million-dollar lottery but lost the ticket on her way to make the claim, then wept openly on the street until a passerby comforted her, pleaded with her to be brave, bought her lunch and insisted that she accept a gift of a hundred dollars. In yet another dream of pathos and violence, my mother discovered a large diamond ring in the back seat of a taxi whose driver then stole it from her, bruised her arm, pushed her out of the cab and sped away.

For all my life my mother lied, from as early, at least, as the time she told me about the eels in the canal. I don't know how old I was when I began to understand the all-important fact that if she lied in such ways as these, then it was not possible for me to trust her in other ways either. Nor do I know how old I was when I began to understand that lies, for my mother, were weapons, or to see the extent to which they revealed how deeply filled with anger and rage she was, carrying despair within the very chambers of her heart. Nor how old when I came at last to perceive the truth about lies, that lies are small wishes for death.

Dressed in shorts and a T-shirt, I spent summer days in my early adolescence taking care of my brother Julian, six years younger than I was. Our grandmother lived with us by then. In the early mornings, before the rest of us were awake, my father would leave for work, taking his black lunch box with him. By the time Julian and I were up for breakfast, my mother would be ready to leave as well. Sometimes we would stand on the front porch to see her off. She walked down the street in the morning sunlight, then at the corner turned toward the station, where she would take the train into the Loop. I watched her as she moved away from us, trim and purposeful and energetic, her handbag tucked under one arm, the strap pulled tightly over her padded shoulder, her narrow skirt flicking back and forth as her legs moved quickly inside it.

I grew to fear the end of the day, when she returned, since this was the time when her anger was the least predictable, the most likely to flare without warning. I tended to become defensive, cautious, and wary, unable to guess what might spark my mother's disapproval and anger, or whether these might appear at all. Sometimes she was merely silent, making the whole family—with the exception, perhaps, of my grandmother—awkward and ill at ease. At other times there were small causes that made her anger flash—I might have broken a cup, or forgotten to put the vacuum cleaner away, or stayed too long at the house of a friend. And on other occasions, responding suddenly to things that had previously gone wholly without comment or note, she would lash out with a malice that seemed only unmotivated and cruel. One night she stood at the stove and began rattling the lids of saucepans unnecessarily, then tossed a spoon so that it clattered noisily into the sink. She was dressed still in a skirt from work and a white blouse with the sleeves pushed up. My father sat at the kitchen table, his hand curled around a bottle of cold beer, Julian on his knee. My mother turned her face toward me where I stood at the back door, leaning against the door frame, looking out through the screen. I was barefoot, and in shorts, wearing a T-shirt. Until only a moment before, I had been unaware of my mother's anger.

"At least put some shreds of clothing over that naked body of yours," she burst out at me. "You look like a street-corner whore."

I went upstairs, to where the stale heat of the day hung heavily in the small rooms. I lay on my bed, pulled my knees up to my chest and laced them there with my arms against the swell of my breasts, wishing that they, and I, would disappear from existence. From the kitchen below, I could hear my mother's raised voice, the clatter of another spoon in the sink, and then the innocently inquiring voice of my grandmother, asking what had happened. Beside me in the unmoving air, the thin white curtains at my window hung as motionlessly and silently as shrouds.

During this period of our lives, the best evenings were those when my mother had a story. Her anger seemed calmed and her spirit congenial when she could improvise at dinner, spinning out the details of a man's heart attack on the train ride home, or a fire of newspapers in one of the cars, or an automobile accident that had happened at noontime, events in which my mother invariably drew attention to herself or played an important part. As always, along with my father, I pretended to believe her, since only harm and unhappiness could result from our failing to do so. This, of course, made of me a liar too. But at that time in my life, as it does even now, it seemed to me that I was unwillingly in possession of a terrible secret about my mother, and that, in order to protect her—to protect us all—from a ruinous and debilitating embarrassment, the results of which could not be imagined, I must not reveal what I knew to anyone, ever.

(In the summer when I stayed at Leonora's farm I slept in an upstairs bedroom with my cousin Sarah. From the darkness outside our window came a nighttime chorus of crickets and frogs, a rising and falling sound that enclosed us like a soft curtain. We slept in Sarah's bed under the weight of only a sheet, our heads on pillows placed side by side. Once late at night I despaired of my fidelity to my mother and family, and I whispered to Sarah in the darkness:

"Does your mother lie?"

"Lie?" she whispered back. I could hear the quick, small rise of anger in her voice. "Why would you ask that?"

Her sharp answer sucked out of me my feeble and wavering courage, and, in a sudden and suffocating fear at the enormity of what I had been about to do, I said something—I don't remember what—to erase my question and quickly blur the subject. Before very much longer I could tell from Sarah's breathing that she had fallen asleep. So I did not submit, at least not yet, to the terrible temptation to betray my mother, and for that I was grateful in part to the right-minded and untroubled Sarah. Just as I was grateful to her mother, who, on the day I was to return home, embraced me tightly and, asking nothing of me and making no test, held me long and hard against her body, as if I were one of her own.)

3

It helps me sometimes if I think of Leonora as a symbol: it helps me if I think of her as being the other side of my mother—the soft side, the side that was not mad, the side that somehow had gotten lost. Leonora's death was the death of the good half of my mother. In this way I can begin to understand more easily my mother's reaction at the news of Leonora's having died—her terrible outburst of anger and unleashed rage. It was her way of fighting that death.

Yet of course I may be entirely wrong. Perhaps my mother did not change. Perhaps, in the confusion and troubled desire of her own precariously balanced life, it was only that, from first to last, she was intolerably jealous of her younger sister, enough so to be spiteful and jealous even of the grief that others felt at her dying. If this were so, then it seems to me now, in some protectively filial and poignantly sorrowful way, that Leonora's death really meant nothing at all. It was of no greater significance than a candle blown out, an eyelid closed, a small twig fallen in the forest.

Somewhere behind Leonora's forehead was a blood vessel that, since the time of her earliest infancy, had possessed a weakness in part of its wall. This weak place, as her life went on, swelled gradually, grew distended, at last came to be puffed out like the membraned throat of a tiny singing frog. Then late one afternoon in August when she was thirty years old it broke. It flooded her brain first with a bruising flow of blood, then quickly, diverting its life, starved it into darkness.

*   *   *

(I was in the house by myself on the evening when the telephone rang and it was my uncle William with the news of Leonora's death. I did not know what to do. When my parents came home forty-five minutes later, I was standing in the doorway between the dining room and the kitchen. They came in through the back door into the kitchen, my father first, carrying a brown sack of groceries, then my mother, after her my grandmother, finally my brother. I remember what happened when I told them. For the first moment no one moved; the four of them stood there motionlessly, looking at me. Then my grandmother sat down slowly on a kitchen chair. She gazed straight ahead, looking at nothing.

"No," she said.

My mother came toward me across the kitchen floor. Then she stopped, and in a quiet voice she said:

"It isn't true. Look at you. What have you been doing? You're lying."

Because I was frightened, and because I was frightened also of her, I stepped backward, and at once I knew that I had made a terrible and irretrievable error, because my movement had in it the appearance of guilt. Tears came to my eyes and, for the first time since William had called, I began crying. It was clear to me that I had done everything wrong.

My mother came closer to me, and her first impulse to anger, verified by my hesitant and backward step, and now feasting on its own certainty, grew suddenly enormous. With a single quick movement she got her hands into my hair and began to shake my head quickly and painfully back and forth. Her face

was contorted in what I took to be anger, but I remember saying to myself over and over, believing the truth of the words:
This is grief. For the first time in your life you are seeing grief.

My mother screamed into my face: "It isn't true! You're
lying, you've always been a liar!" I struggled with my own fingers against the tangled grip of hers, but they were like roots
and I was unable to loosen them. It seemed to me a very long
time, long enough to wish to die several times over of humilia-
tion and grief and sorrow, before my father, having dropped
his bag of groceries onto the kitchen table, was able to pry my
mother's fingers from my hair and, holding her arms against her
sides from behind, draw her away from me. I turned and fled,
hearing behind me the wreckage and chaos of voices and sobs.

This happened in August of 1954, when I was thirteen years
old. Later we did not speak of it in the family, but, however
inexplicably, went on living as if the incident had not happened. That was to become and remain our habit, pretending
with painstaking care, as time continued to draw us through
our lives, that nothing had happened. Perhaps we—I most of
all—had no choice in this. I think now, after all, that what my
mother wanted at that terrible moment in the kitchen doorway
was to kill me.)

4

It seems to me very simple now to understand what it was
that captivated me about Leonora: in her presence, I needed to
feel no fear. Leonora made no unusual or mysteriously chang-

ing demands as the price for her affection; I believe in fact that she set no price for it at all, and this seemed to me exotic and wonderful, although at the age of twelve I very likely would have been unable—or afraid—to explain why it seemed especially so. I was accustomed to being uncertain and deceived and betrayed in my affections, and, to my great comfort and wonder, I learned that such was not to be the nature of things during the time I spent on the farm. It became clear to me that Leonora's kindness could be trusted unquestionably, and so, quite simply, in a way that I suppose was halfway a secret even from myself, I fell in love with Leonora.

Even at this distance, the words force me into exaggeration. I was fond of Leonora, it is true, and perhaps even infatuated by her for a time. With something fresh and uncomplicated about her, and above all with something steady and consistent, she was a relief to me, a relief welcome and intense enough that for a time perhaps it did burst into love, or into what I have called by that word.

And yet when I think of Leonora now, I find that I think no more—perhaps because I know no more—of the woman herself than I do of the farm where she lived. The place itself has stayed in my memory vividly, however much that place may in fact be heightened and colored in my feelings by the remembered presence of Leonora. Yet even here my memory challenges me, and I find myself, at the distance of almost three decades, seeing poverty and squalor in details that, when I was a child, seemed to me to be comforting and familiar and homely and filled with ease. That the yard at the back of the house, for example, was worn away to bare dirt, wandered over each morning and afternoon by William's dozen head of sheep, and off and on throughout the day by some of Leonora's scratching pullets. That the rusted pickup truck and the family car were parked on the dirt under the shade of an elm, dripping black oil from their undersides inches from the house, or that the back porch had lost its center supports, so that the roof sagged and the sunken floor rested its drooping lower lip on the hard-packed dirt. In the bare kitchen, cracked yellow linoleum on the floor, a refrigerator door roughened to the touch by pocks of spreading rust, and on an empty wall a drugstore calendar hanging desolately from a driven nail.

(I remember the quietness of things, the steadiness of them, the redolence of the sun-warmed countryside in the summer air, and the varied scents of the farm. The peacefulness of that summer season. In the mornings William milked his cows before breakfast, helped by Sarah's younger brother, and sometimes Sarah and I watched them, or sat to warm ourselves in the sunlight on the plank fence outside the barn, or helped sweep out the cows' stalls, or at the end took the silver kitchen jug of yesterday's milk from where it hung on a hook in the cooler, submerged there to its neck in cold moving water, and carried it back to the house where we watched Leonora skim half the cream into a pitcher, stir the rest back in, and then pour the three tall glasses on the table full of milk. Cool sunlight outdoors, coming through the green leaves of the elms, and sheep walking casually past the windows. In the mornings cool air seemed to drift through the house, and Leonora folded down the sheets on the beds to let them freshen, with the windows thrown open wide. She wore men's blue shirts with the loose sleeves turned up two or three times at the cuffs, and long cotton skirts of close-patterned fabric in bright, plumage-like colors of blue or red or green or yellow. The way to find Leonora during the day was to look for the flash of bright color—as she stood up in the midday sunlight from among the rows of the garden, or stepped out of the doorway of the milk shed, or, late in the afternoon, walked through the lengthening shadows of the yard with a woven basket on her arm toward the coop where her layers nested. Often at this time Sarah and I would scramble out of a tree or come out of the edge of the woods where we might be playing and run after her, catching up with her at the door to the chicken coop, where her hand rested already on the latch. *Don't run so,* she would tell us. *You'll scare them and they'll flutter like all pandemonium.* Then she would open the door slowly and bend her head to go in and Sarah and I would follow her into the hot, close air inside, and the three of us would feel with our hands inside the rows of straw-filled boxes hung along the walls, burrowing sometimes under the plump hot feathers of a hen herself who refused to give up her place, and we would draw out the smooth eggs, many of them still warm, and put them carefully in the bottom of Leonora's basket while the fat layers with their yellow legs and long splayed toes cocked their small heads at us, looking out of one suspicious eye and then the other, or strutted archly around the floor of the coop and clucked their offended and disapproving clucks at our intrusion.

Most things about the working of the farm I don't know, or don't remember. Whether Leonora sold her eggs to the cross-roads store in Alma, or to a dealer in eggs, or to neighboring farmers. Who bought William's milk, the two or three silver cans of it submerged in the slowly moving water in the cooler in the milk shed, or how often they bought it. Why he kept his flock of sheep, or what he did with their wool in the spring, or how much money it could have been worth. I was a child, I lived in a town near the city and on the edge of the prairie, and the farm down south near the river seemed to me a mysteriously comfortable place that was able, if needed at all, to explain itself. It did not occur to me to ask questions. And so now, decades later, I know very little about the commerce of the farm, but what I remember instead are the scents, the moods, and the quietness. I remember the yellow linoleum in the kitchen, with the color worn away to the dull brown second layer in front of the sink and stove. I remember the white oilcloth on the table, its webbings of thread showing through at the worn corners where it bent to hang down. I remember the times of the day that were the quietest. The gray of dawn when the birds were first beginning to sound. The long dead hour in the heart of the afternoons, when the only sound was the slow rising song of the cicada, and then its plummeting fall. And that period of time in the evenings after supper when the dishes were done and William had finished the milking and the barn was swept and the cows had wandered in a long single file back out to the pasture for the night, and darkness was gathering, with the light falling swiftly out of the air, and when the crickets and frogs and insects in the grass and woods hadn't yet begun to raise their nighttime chorus. I remember the distant barking of a dog at this time of the evening from a neighboring farm toward the river, and then the sudden answering bark of Sarah's black dog outside the kitchen window in the yard, until William went outdoors and told him to be quiet and spent

some time, as he usually did, sitting against a post on the edge
of the sagging porch and smoking a cigar in the darkness, its
ash growing a brighter red from time to time when he drew
on it. I remember climbing into bed in Sarah's upstairs room
with its bare wooden floor and slanted ceiling and curtained
window, the air close and warm from the sun having fallen all
afternoon against the pitch of the roof just over our heads. And
I remember, too, Leonora coming into our room each night
on her own way to bed. Sometimes, when Sarah was already
asleep, I would pretend to be sleeping too, and Leonora would
lean over the bed, her face near mine, and touch each of our
foreheads with her hand, pushing our hair gently away from
our faces. This moment came to be an important one for me,
as if in some way it were a secret that no one knew about other
than me. I would watch Leonora go out of the room toward the
dim light from the hallway, and then that light would go out
as well and I would lie in the darkness listening to the chorus
of sounds coming in through the window from outdoors. It
seemed to me as I lay there falling into sleep after having been
touched by Leonora that I was at the very center of all things,
precisely where I might most wish to be. The old farmhouse
was like an unmoving point from which everything else in the
world radiated outward, and it seems to me now that I would
fall asleep each night thinking of the dark fields around me
cooling slowly in the night air, of the dirt road winding its
way toward the smoothly flowing river, of fields beyond those
fields, rivers beyond that river, all in the quietness of the summer night, the gentle arms of the republic reaching softly and
securely outward to the seas.)

* * *

When William called the next summer and I picked up the telephone in Three Islands, the connection crackled with static, and his voice, carried on a weakened current, sounded distant and muffled and small. Hearing his voice this way, through a bad long-distance connection on a rural line, made the farm seem a thousand miles away, on the far side of the world, more distant and more unreachable than I could imagine.

Now, years later, I think of that telephone call and I am able to imagine my uncle William standing in the kitchen of the farmhouse and speaking into the telephone where it is mounted on the wall beside the screen door. Beyond the door is the sagging back porch, and beyond the porch is the empty yard, with evening shadows lengthening across it.

Leonora died late in the afternoon, at a time when Sarah and her brother were in one of the outlying fields with William, helping him as he loaded bales of new hay onto a flatbed wagon drawn behind the tractor. That the rural homeliness of her sudden death—she died inside the chicken house, as she gathered eggs—may have had something about it of the ludicrous or the bathetic was an idea that did not occur to me at the time, and hardly since. Leonora was safely removed for me from the touch of any macabre or rustic comedy, however strong the temptation to see it may have been to others. Much of what I did feel at first, I remember, in the sentiment and particular confusion of my own thirteen years, was pity that she had been alone at the time of her death, and sorrow that her death had gone undiscovered for the hour or two that it had.

The doctor said that she had died instantly—"in her tracks,"

I heard my father repeat the phrase. The doctor explained—whether only to comfort the family, I don't know—that she fell just as she would have fallen if struck by a great blow to the back of the head. For a long time I wondered about this, and a picture of Leonora at the moment of her death formed itself in my mind and stayed with me for years afterward. In this image, Leonora stood bent forward at the waist, reaching into one of the rows of wooden nests fastened to the wall. Of this much of the image I felt quite certain, but other things prevented me from completing the picture entirely, or from bringing it into final form. I did not know, for example, whether the wicker basket on Leonora's arm with the kitchen towel folded into its bottom was filled with eggs at the moment of her death, or whether it was empty. If it was full, I did not know whether the eggs were broken when she fell, or whether, perhaps, they had rolled out safely onto the straw-covered floor of the hen house. I did not know—in spite of the doctor's words—whether Leonora lowered herself gently, almost as if she were lying down on the ground to sleep, or whether she was seized in sudden agony by the great internal blow and straightened up, with astonishment and horror on her face, attempted perhaps to walk outdoors, and then fell awkwardly and terribly to the floor. I did not know whether the white hens cocked their heads in curiosity, looking first out of one eye and then the other, or whether, frightened by the suddenness, the sound, the flash of color, they fluttered up in pandemonium, filling the air with dust and with the frightened beating of their wings.

Later, even as late as my years in college, I had a recurring dream in which I stood looking at her where she lay dead. In this dream she lay peacefully on her side, as if she might have been asleep, with one arm extended upward, her head resting on it as if on a pillow. Her eyes were closed. Her full skirt, of a bright yellow cotton, lay as if she might have straightened it before sleeping. She wore a cloth band in her hair. One lock had found its way free and lay over her forehead.

In the dream, I was alone on the farm. I left the chicken coop and went to the farmhouse and, in the warm afternoon silence of an upstairs bedroom, I changed into my best clothes, as if I were about to leave on a trip. Then I went back to the chicken coop, let myself in through the wooden door, closed it behind me, and stood gazing down at Leonora where she lay on the floor. The white hens walked idly near her, now and then stepping across her ankles. One of them perched for a time on the swell of her hip under the yellow skirt, cocked its head, then spread its wings and jumped down. I do not remember that I wept. I stood gazing at her, dressed in my traveling clothes, for what seemed a time not intended to have any end; but then somehow, in the dream, I was also standing in the doorway of the farmhouse kitchen, looking in through the screen door. The house was empty and silent in the deep hush of the late afternoon. On the table in the middle of the room stood a colander of green beans and three or four red tomatoes, intended, I suppose, for dinner, resting where Leonora had placed them on her way from the garden, going out to gather the eggs.

5

That is, of course, the end of that story. The part that remains, the more difficult part, is about my mother and me.

What happened, it seems to me now, is that for forty-five

minutes in my childhood I went mad—for those three quarters of an hour between the time of William's telephone call with the news of Leonora's death and the time of my parents' coming home through the back door into the kitchen.

It seemed to me during those minutes that there was nothing I could do. And yet it seemed that I must do something. And everything I did was wrong.

I remember the enormity of the silence in the house around me after I hung up the telephone. In sudden fear I wondered if I had imagined William's voice, or if possibly I had misunderstood him. Perhaps I had heard incorrectly what he said. Or perhaps there had not been any call.

But of course there had. Yet nothing in the unchanged house around me was able to prove to me that this was the case. I was unable to trust my senses, to believe what I was being asked to believe, and yet it was absolutely imperative that I do so.

I went into the kitchen, where the book I had been reading when the telephone rang lay face down on the table. Leonora had been dead when I sat there reading a few minutes before. But it was different now because I knew that she was dead and had not known then. I could not sit down at the table once again, tuck my bare feet under me on the padded chair, and continue to read. It seemed to me that there was nothing in the world that I could do just as I had done before.

I walked through the rooms of the house, through the dining room past the black telephone where it rested on its stand at the base of the stairs, through the living room, and went out the front door onto the stoop. I sat down on the top step in the evening light. But I could not sit there either, wearing my shorts and T-shirt, as if nothing were different from before. I remember that across the street a man mowed his front lawn, pushing the mower ahead of him with the quiet well-oiled whir of the spinning blade.

I went back through the rooms of the house, the living room, the dining room, then into the kitchen, where I stood looking out through the open back door. Nothing in the house behind me moved. I wondered again whether the telephone had really rung or whether I had really heard William's voice. I went into the front hallway and opened the closet door and looked at the jackets and winter coats hanging there. In the dining room I pulled open drawers and looked at the folded linens inside, then closed them. I do not believe I knew why I was doing any of these things. I am not certain that I was thinking at all, except to think: *I am doing these things*. In the kitchen I opened the cupboards and looked at the dishes resting inside, then closed them. The linoleum floor was cool against my bare feet. I opened the utensil drawer and took out my mother's large carving knife. I touched my thumb to the sharp edge of its curved blade. I raised it to my mouth and put the tip of my tongue against the flat of the blade, leaving a small round spot of dampness on the dark metal, and then I touched the sharp edge to the side of my face, against cheek and cheekbone, and held it there steadily, with a soft, scarcely felt pressure. Afterward I put the knife back in the drawer, pushed the drawer closed, and, as if moved at last by a sense of purpose, I went upstairs to my room and pulled off my T-shirt and shorts and tossed them onto my bed. In my drawer I found a pair of knee socks and hurried them on, as well as a half slip. From hangers in my closet I took a fresh white blouse and pleated skirt and put them on, and I slipped into my polished school loafers and put a barrette in each side of my hair, and then I went into my parents' bedroom to look at myself in the large mirror over my mother's dressing table. I moved as far away as I was able, against the wall, in order to see as much of myself as I could. I bent my knees slightly and pulled my skirt out at the sides to see that it hung evenly, then turned sideways as well, peering as I did so into the mirror. From my mother's crowded dressing table—I was aware by this time of a pressing sense of urgency—I took a lipstick and mascara and a jar of rouge and returned to my own room where I sat at my desk and, peering into the small mirror propped there, hurried to make up my face.

What I might have done if my parents and brother and grandmother had not returned home at this time, I don't know. Whether I would really have left the house and begun to search, somehow, for a means of traveling southward from Three Islands toward Leonora's farm—I don't know this either. Certainly I do not remember having formed any concrete plans about how I would travel, exactly what I would do when I went out of the house, although this in itself probably means little. I understand now that my actions had about them the logic of actions in a dream. As in a dream, each thing that I did seemed at the time to have a reason of its own, some internal purpose and rightness that had nothing to do with its outside consequence, and, precisely as in such a dream, it was by this feeling alone that I was moved and propelled.

The sound of my parents' car turning into the driveway was like an awakening from that previous scheme of things, a jarring into a different consciousness, and, sitting at my desk in my room, I understood immediately the enormity of my miscalculation, the wrongness of everything I had done, and the extent, without hope of escape, to which I had doomed myself to being wholly misunderstood. I should at this very moment have been running out to the arriving car, pushed along by a heedless urgency; I should have been deluging my family with the terrible, unutterable news of Leonora's death. But instead they were going to find me indoors, in my best clothes, with my face ludicrously made up, as if I had been playing grownup, frolicking as in carefree child's play in the face of a death that I appeared to care nothing about. Better than to be discovered in this way would be for me to hide silently in my room and say nothing, or flee the house through the front door and escape altogether. But of course I could do neither of those things. I was the only one who knew that Leonora was dead. I alone possessed the awesome burden of that knowledge. It was essential—of course it was essential; it was imperative—that I tell the others.

In my room, I tore at my clothing, already hearing the car doors slamming in the back yard. But this was foolish, I had no time to change my clothes. I pulled my skirt back up, buttoned one or two buttons of my blouse, rushed across the hallway to the bathroom and wet a washcloth under the spout. I rubbed it once across my face, sideways, pressing down with all my strength, as if to wash my face itself away. Then I ran downstairs, two steps at a time. I heard their voices as they talked casually among themselves, and the rattle of someone's hand on the metal latch of the screen door. I was still holding the washcloth.

That was how I came to be standing in the doorway of the kitchen when they came in. I held a wet washcloth in one hand.

My clothing was in disarray. I presented to them a child's face that was askew, out of joint, insane: my eyes, against heavily rouged cheeks, were great smears of blackness, and my mouth was a sideways gash of bright red, as if it had been bloodied by the passing knuckles of an iron hand.

My voice, to my great astonishment, quavered only very slightly. I told my family, as calmly as I could, that William had called; that Leonora was dead; that she had died in the chicken house, in the afternoon, gathering eggs.

I told the truth. I did not lie.

6

The almost three decades that have passed since then have given me, if nothing else, a certain time to think over these events. Perhaps I understand them no better now than I did when I was a child. Perhaps I am intended never to understand them entirely. And yet some aspects of them seem to me more clear. It seems to me quite likely now, for example, that what I experienced at learning of Leonora's death was grief—but grief with no vocabulary, grief perhaps without my knowing even what it was, certainly without my knowing before that moment what very great depths it could spring from. I needed in some way to pay homage to Leonora, but that homage— partly because, in the terrible forced secrecy of my feelings, I felt it to be forbidden; partly because I was frightened—took the form of what seems to me now to have been a brief madness. And perhaps, for that matter, I did lie to my mother, although, once again, I did so through no will of my own. Perhaps I lied to her in the doorway to the kitchen by not saying, partly because at that time I still did not understand it fully: *I feel as if my mother has died.*

And I still wonder, too, if my mother's rage was not caused by her seeing in my twisted face the truth of this fact; if what she saw, in her awareness of her own terrible abandonment, was not the loss of all those things in her life that she was never to have.

My dream of Leonora, as I have said, stayed with me for years with little change. Always I stood dressed in my finest clothes, and always I gazed down at her body where it lay as if she were sleeping, with—so it seems to me now—the basket of unbroken eggs resting beside her. Around me, radiating outward, was invariably the quiet stillness of the farm.

As for the canal, and my dreams of travel and escape and flight, a small incident stays with me from near that time. My father chose frequently, after his evening meal, to walk outdoors, and sometimes I went with him. One warm evening in the spring, I went with him to the tobacconist's, where he bought a cigar, then strolled with him back along the street, past the front of our own house, and into the small park along the edge of the canal, where my mother had once told me about the eels. My father leaned with his arms resting on the rail, and I stood beside him. A barge was passing, and, as it moved by, one of the crew members walked along the deck toward the stern. He seemed to be getting nowhere, but, as the barge moved under his feet, he hung in one spot directly in front of us, within easy reach of a shout. My father laughed, waved his cigar with a brief gesture of his hand, and called out:

"Hey! You're not getting anywhere! You've got to run faster!"

Seizing my father's light humor, the man clenched his fists, grinning toward us, and did a mime's imitation of a hard run. He struggled, pumped his arms, and still got nowhere, remaining suspended in the same spot in the warm evening air in front of where my father and I stood at the rail, with only the mammoth, whalelike bulk of the barge sliding easily and slowly past underneath his feet.

I think of it now as an image of time coming somehow to a stop: as it had come somehow to a stop when I heard of Leonora's death; as it would do again, five years later, when I stood at the door of my parents' bedroom and looked in, helplessly and in a naïve terror, at what I saw clearly for the first time to be my own absence; as it was to do much later still, when my poor mother, through a final effort of inestimable courage and despair, was to draw me with her one last and unmerciful and pitiable time into a poisoned and time-stopped sea.

II

THREE ISLANDS, ILLINOIS

SLEEPING

I

My maternal grandmother, on a quiet summer morning in 1947, came for what was to be a temporary visit with my family, then in the end stayed for the remainder of her life. I was six years old at the time. I remember the moment of her arrival clearly.

Our street was not a through street but came to a dead end at the bank of the canal, making it quieter and less frequently traveled than others nearby. My mother had told me to wait for my grandmother on the front steps of our house, and I did so. Sunlight came down through the leaves of trees and fell in broken, water-lily pools on the sidewalk and street.

After I had waited for some time, a car, driven by my uncle Victor, went slowly past our house, turned around at the empty lot by the canal, then came back and stopped at our curb. A door opened and my grandmother, her feet and legs appearing first, stepped out.

My uncle Victor stayed in the car. As if he were in a great hurry, he reached behind the front seat to open the back door and push two bags toward the edge of the seat for my grandmother to take from him. When she had done this, he pulled both doors closed and after leaning over to exchange some words with my grandmother through the open window, he drove away. His black car went down the street past the first intersection and then on to the next, where suddenly it turned left. With a single wink of red taillights, it disappeared from sight, darting away as if escaping furtively through a small invisible opening among distant green trees.

The long-ago moment of my grandmother's arrival at our house has stayed in my memory for a great number of years, and I have come to think of it, with its fleeting array of symbols and its place as a dividing point in the history of my family, as an early moment when I saw time itself breaking in two, the pieces falling away from one another forever.

My grandmother that morning, like a fragment of history washed up on our shore, stood at the curb looking toward me, and I sat on the steps looking back. The hem of the dress she wore, as it always did, hung lower in front than in back, and her body seemed to sag with a familiar forlorn air from the weight of the suitcase she held in one hand, and of the old-fashioned bag of embroidered cloth that hung from the other. Next to her on the curb, leaning as if about to fall, waited a second large suitcase.

Of course I left the steps of the house and went to her, even though my feelings toward my grandmother were uncertain ones. She was not a naturally affectionate woman, and I know that in my early childhood I always feared and disliked her slightly.

·

When I was younger still, I remember my mother explaining to me, with no surrounding context that has stayed in my mind: "Your grandmother is a widow." I am not certain whether I heard the whisper of death in the word at that time, although I know that by then I had already been taken more than once to visit my grandfather's grave. My grandfather's death—in 1938, sudden and unexpected—was one of the series of shattering events that had fallen upon my mother's family beginning near the middle 1930s, events having as one of their end results, among others, the appearance of my grandmother a decade or so later at the end of our front sidewalk.

During the later years of World War II, when my father was in Hawaii, my grandmother had lived by herself in a tiny apartment downtown, above the main street of Three Islands. My mother took me there numerous times to visit, bundling me first—I remember the journeys as taking place in winter—in coat and hat and mittens. We made the trip by trolley car. In the years immediately after the war the trolleys were to disappear from Three Islands, their iron tracks paved over without trace, but I remember standing on a street corner with my mother, dirty banks of snow piled nearby, and watching the trolley appear slowly around a curve, then stopping to pick us up.

The building my grandmother lived in had fixed to its side an outdoor wooden staircase with open risers, which frightened me as we climbed up, since it seemed to me an easy matter to slip through the gaping stair backs into the sea of open air

below. A dimly lighted corridor extended through the center
of the building upstairs. Finding the right door in the gloom,
my mother rapped with her knuckles, and my grandmother,
after a delay, would open the door of her apartment the merest
crack, the width of a single eye, and peer out at us for a moment
before opening it further.

In my grandmother's kitchen, windowless and at the back
of her apartment, my mother and my grandmother sat across
from one another, coffee cups placed on the small table between them. My mother held a cigarette in her hand, as usual,
and its smoke rose up into the metal shade of the lamp that
hung suspended over the table. While they sat there, I stood in
the other room (there were only two) and looked out through
one of the tall windows, where it seemed to me a strange thing
to look down on the tops of cars parked diagonally at the curb
below, and, instead of trees or hedges, to see storefronts across
the street with displays of merchandise in their windows, and
people coming in and out of the doorways.

My grandmother had a job clerking at Schroeder's Department Store, just downstairs from her apartment and in the
same building, and perhaps that is part of the reason she remained there as long as she did instead of coming to stay with
us sooner—when my father was away, for example, before my
brother Julian was born, and when only my mother and I were
living in our house. There were severities of baffled pride buried
within my mother's family, though, and conflict, and a confused tradition of self-reliance, all of which must have played a
role. But there were also commanding and deeply rooted mat-

ters of money, and the pervasive question, too, of my uncle Victor's suspected criminality.

These things all come to me as if from an infinitely remote and faintly known past, by the meager fragments of innuendo and echo: my grandfather's losing his job on the railroad in 1936, and taking work afterward as a golf caddy; his sudden death two years later, leaving my grandmother with two daughters, two increasingly unreliable sons, and no money; the dreaded conversion of the family home into a boardinghouse, offering room and board to laboring men; my mother, then seventeen, dropping out of high school to take on night shifts in the telephone building downtown by the canal.

.

As for my uncle Victor, the general understanding is that when he arranged for the sale of the family house, early in 1941, he did so in such a way as to divert the proceeds both from my grandmother herself and from his own siblings, although some of the money (this, like much else, remains unclear) may have found its way to his older brother Calvin. For some time Victor supported his mother by paying the rent on her apartment downtown. When this practice came to an end, his own supply of money having mysteriously disappeared in its entirety, the time seemed right to consider other arrangements— and it was then, in what was ostensibly a temporary measure, that my grandmother came to stay with us.

A wastrel and inexplicably directionless, my uncle Victor was to die—in Wyoming, of alcoholic breakdown—sometime during the summer only two years after he brought my grandmother to our house. Why he went West I do not know, but

I have always imagined him, in death, lying as if comfortably asleep on the flank of a distant foothill under breeze-touched pines. I of course scarcely knew him, but I know that my mother felt toward her doomed brother a contradictory and fierce loyalty, one that allowed her the privilege of condemning and maligning him, but that, although with some modifications and exceptions, brought her most bitter wrath down upon the heads of others—including my grandmother—who took it upon themselves to do the same.

I suppose that I think of Uncle Victor as one of my few actual glimpses of a long and distant past otherwise wholly lost to me, and I still remember his black car disappearing suddenly through green foliage at the far end of our street, as if drawing behind it, like an actor's cape, the last vestiges of all the history that had gone before. As for the house he sold, I saw that with my own eyes as well, although I was then only four, when it was being put up on jacks and transferred to a long truck to be carried away entirely. In my mind's eye, however, I still see it clearly as it was before: white, square, unshaded by trees in high afternoon sunlight, with bedsheets hanging thickly on lines out in the back, toward the canal.

II

Our own house was modest and small, with hardly sufficient room in it for my grandmother as well as for ourselves. When she first arrived, my brother Julian had been born only for a number of weeks, and for some time he continued to sleep in my parents' bedroom, first in his bassinet and then in his crib, while my grandmother was moved into the small extra room immediately across the upstairs hallway from my own. When Julian grew older, however, passing his second birthday, this arrangement was soon changed, and my grandmother's small room was given to Julian instead. My grandmother, there being no other place for her to go, crossed the hall and brought her possessions into my room with me.

When my grandmother came to join me in this way, I had just passed my own ninth birthday. The two of us were to remain sleeping partners for slightly over three years, when at last my father expanded our house, which he had spoken of doing for some time, by converting half of the attic into a room for my grandmother that could be reached by way of the narrow wooden steps that rose from behind a door at one end of the upstairs hallway.

My father covered the exposed rafters of the sloping attic ceiling, covered the uprights of the low walls in the same way, and put finishing material on the floor. At the window, my mother hung curtains that she had sewn by hand, of light blue cotton gathered together and held open with ties at their middles. With the help of a neighbor, my father carried a narrow bed for my grandmother up to the new room, followed by a mirrored dresser. A small table went as well, and a rocking chair accompanied by a small footstool that was upholstered in heavy material with a needlework design. A length of iron pipe set across a corner at one end of the room demarcated my grandmother's closet, hidden from view by a blanketlike curtain that could be drawn closed on wooden rings. A wooden partition with a latched door separated my grandmother's room from the other end of the attic, where clotheslines were strung from hooks in the walls, and where in the winter months my mother hung up sheets and laundry to dry.

Once the room was finished, I entered it only rarely. There were occasions, naturally enough, when I went into the attic to set piles of freshly folded laundry on my grandmother's bed, when my grandmother herself wasn't at home to do this work; and from time to time (especially in the somewhat later years, when my mother had returned to full-time work, taking an early train each morning into Chicago) I carried the vacuum cleaner up the narrow stairway in order to sweep my grandmother's floor and clean the braided scatter rug that lay between her dresser and bed.

The small room itself was pleasant, and I find myself now, after many years, thinking of it in terms that are peculiarly associative and abstract, having to do mainly with emptiness and the quiet, museumlike absence of time. I imagine my grandmother, for example, sitting in her rocking chair through long, chill, gray winter afternoons, gradually decomposing into harmlessly drifting curls of dust on the floor, which I then, some bright Saturday morning in late springtime, draw into the hose of the vacuum cleaner, wondering idly in a distant corner of my mind where my grandmother has gone.

.

It is interesting to me that an image of this sort, of insubstantial and weightless dust, should remain with me now, since in the formative years when she slept with me in my own room downstairs I was made so clearly aware of the weight-possessing intimacies of my grandmother's body. I do not believe my grandmother ever to have been an especially intelligent woman, and her careless immodesty before me, in the years of my own adolescent awakening, may have been due to nothing more than the deaf and mute oblivion of thoughtlessness. But it was impossible for me not to feel that in seeing my grandmother's nakedness a stern judgment was being forced upon me and that I was being made to see what I myself was inevitably destined to become. It was not always possible for me to contrive a way to be out of the room at moments of intimacy, and, when my grandmother casually dressed and undressed before me, I found myself often unable to avoid observing, with a curious fascination and frightened revulsion at one and the same time, the downcast eyes of her pathetic, drooping breasts, the upturned cradle of her pelvis, with its jutting wing-bones poised like great birds over the withering darkness between her legs, the wrinkled and shadow-gathering flesh that descended below.

.

From as early as I can remember her, my grandmother preferred to sleep a great deal, arranging to take naps in the afternoon, whenever that was possible, and choosing to go to bed most often at an early hour. I had a small bed lamp in whose narrow light (I lay propped on one arm, my back toward my reclining grandmother) I would often read until I sensed that the rest of the house had fallen into sleep around me. If I looked over at the other side of the bed before turning out the light, I would often see there the startling image of my grandmother in the early stages of her sleep. She would lie on her back, her head flung against the pillow, her mouth a great cavern of openness as if she had struggled to emit one last scream or to take in a final, sustaining breath before being throttled into lifelessness by the strong and bony hands of death. Her throat, exposed, offered itself to whatever being or force might steal into the room through the darkness to bring her end, and her gray hair, loosened for the night, would be flung outward across her pillow as if in a radiating and shadowy nimbus of terror and alarm and grief.

Yet if for some reason I were to awaken in the later and more profound depths of the night and look over once again at my grandmother, I would as often find her sleeping peacefully, lying on her side, curled under the blankets with her knees drawn up in a childlike posture that made her seem small, harmless, and frail, her placidly resting face illuminated faintly by the dim light from the street lamp that came in steadily and silently at the window of my room.

.

I have often pondered the unflagging strength of my mother's desire to provide my grandmother with a home: a sustained and turbulent desire that for many years I believed had to do only with my mother's great wish for respectability and order.

It would have been quite possible, in the beginning, for my grandmother to have moved in with my uncle Calvin and his first wife instead of with us, although my mother's point was borne out, especially as the years passed, that her life there would have been more deeply visited by a continued and clinging poverty—and in some ways by squalor—than proved to be the case at our house.

My mother must have considered our house from the start to be the most natural and suitable choice, and herself to be the sibling—as the older of the two daughters—who should by obligation and right provide my grandmother with a place to live. I remember the period when there was discussion of my grandmother's moving to southern Illinois to live with Leonora and her family: my mother argued strongly against it, relying as usual on my father's pliable and customary willingness to acquiesce to her wishes. As a result, except for visits elsewhere from time to time, my grandmother stayed with us uninterruptedly.

But the relationship was an uneasy one between my mother and my grandmother, marked throughout the years of my growing up not only by my mother's kindness but also by her easily released and frequent outbursts of rage. For some time, I believed that my mother's anger was the result only of a deep chagrin at the fact of my grandmother's homely shabbiness, and of a pained embarrassment at her commonly thoughtless and unselfconscious behavior.

That my mother's reactions were inconsistent and unpredictable, however, made it only more difficult to understand them. Sometimes her anger appeared suddenly, without warning; at other times, when there seemed to be cause, it remained inexplicably quiescent. There were occasions, for example, when my grandmother's eccentricities and lapses—sleeping past the time when she was to have put in a roast; setting out for her job at Schroeder's Department Store with the back of her dress unbuttoned and her white slip visible through the yawning gap (my mother, as if she were dressing a child, would tug roughly at the sides of the cloth as she did up the buttons)—would draw from my mother only gentle admonishments or, at the very worst, impatient sighs of reproval.

There were other times, however, when a deeper current was touched, perhaps when tension existed already between the two, or when something more profound was awakened within my mother. It was possible then for quarrels of great intensity suddenly to begin, building quickly from raised voices to shouted threats, to the throwing of objects, and at last to the flinging of recriminations that reached deeply, like pale tendrils, back into the lost and ruined history of my mother's family.

It could be, perhaps, that my grandmother had embarrassingly shuffled to the corner store early one morning in only her bedroom slippers and robe, or had gone unthinkingly to the post office with her uncovered hair in curlers; had innocently confided something to a curious neighbor at the front curb that was not the neighbor's to know; or, above all, in a moment of carelessness or anger, fleeting ingratitude, or frustration at the confusion of life with my mother, had let fall from her lips a derogatory or comparative remark about the suspect and devious character of my uncle Victor, or about his surviving brother Calvin, or even something of a veiled but critical nature about my long-dead grandfather himself: small wounds, tiny nicks in the sleeping flesh of time that were hardly noticeable to others, but that pierced my mother to the quick of her being, causing her to bleed profusely in rage and despair.

·

As the years went by in our life together, my grandmother retired more frequently to her room in the attic and spent increasingly long hours there. Often, during periods of stress, she would disappear discreetly and unnoticed at the earliest signs of a gathering quarrel; at other times, when she might have misjudged the atmosphere, or have waited too long, or been taken entirely by surprise, it was as if she were chased up into the attic, a fluttering gray figure blown weightlessly up the stairs on the turbulent wind of my mother's displeasure.

Her room was immediately above mine, and her bed was placed directly over my own, where I sometimes imagined her lying like a second image of myself, floating a certain distance above me in our simultaneous but unshared sleep. Sometimes when I came home from school and did not know she was there, in the middle part of the afternoon when the house was otherwise empty, I would be made conscious of her presence by the muffled creak of a floorboard, or by the sound of a shoe falling to the floor as she dropped it from the bed, lying down for her nap. There were times when the sound of the other shoe never came, although I sat at my desk waiting, so swiftly did she plunge into sleep.

Like my grandmother, I spent long hours in my room. I did my homework there, often took short naps in the very late afternoon before my parents came home from work, and I continued my habit of reading secretly late into the night. Sometimes, especially during the cool, wonderfully changing weather of autumn or spring, I did a strange thing which I confided to no one. I fell into the habit of opening my window a narrow crack and then for some time kneeling or sitting on the floor beside it. There, I pressed my nose to the small opening and breathed in the fresh, mysterious air that I imagined as coming to me alone like a secret and private gift from distances farther and farther away: from the rolling fields of the prairie reaching off to the west; from the remote, sparsely pine-grown mountains where my uncle Victor lay asleep on his hillside; from across the invisible sea itself, whose icy scent I imagined I smelled; and from even farther, carrying to me the faintly sweet and cinnamoned breath of the exotic, most distant shores of the world.

A NOTEBOOK OF MY GRANDFATHER

I

For most of his life, my maternal grandfather worked on the railroad: as a brakeman when he was young, then for many years in the freight and switching yards in Three Islands. Although he died two and a half years before I was born, the long period of my own growing up was governed overwhelmingly by his presence.

And yet even so, because so many years have passed and because I never saw him, he comes to me only in silence, in fragments and wordless echoes that are themselves like small broken pieces of time.

II

By the time I reached high school, or certainly by the time I left home for college, the freight yards in Three Islands were almost entirely inactive and abandoned. As a younger child, however, every day I would hear the rumbling and muffled crashing of freight cars being assembled into trains that would then set out across the plains toward the far West. The sound came to our house from far on the other side of Three Islands, and I remember it now as a pleasant and evocative sound that I associate particularly with summer evenings, when the air was perfectly calm and people could talk from one front porch to another without raising their voices, or with nights deep in the heart of winter, when the brittle and frozen air carried sounds great distances. In my adolescence, I often yearned idly for the distant places and times portrayed in the books I read, and, lying in my bed, I would sometimes imagine that from the freight yards far across town I was hearing the distant, booming sound of guns in battle, or ice breaking up on a great northern river, or the sound of avalanches, triggered by thawing winds, sliding with muffled thunder down neighboring mountain passes.

III

Most vividly, images come to me from my grandfather's early years. I think, for example, of dry summer heat and blue sky, and a train rushing across a great prairie that is covered to the horizons with ripening grain, dried by the heat of the sun into a gently undulating sea of dusty yellow.

The train is traveling westward. My grandfather makes his way precariously along the tops of the hurtling wooden boxcars; or I see him climbing the iron ladder up the side of one of them; or he stands on the rear platform of the caboose, lounging at the rail, watching the tracks speed by beneath him and recede gradually into a remote and faraway point.

For whatever reason, I do not see other trainmen in these re-curring scenes: stokers or fellow brakemen, for example, who might share meals with my grandfather in the caboose, sleep there, or play cards, or stand with him at the rail. The single exception to this is the engineer. Sometimes I briefly glimpse his cocked elbow on the ledge of his open window and the up-tilted brim of his striped cap as he leans out into the stream of air alongside the locomotive to peer ahead down the onrushing tracks.

IV

Everything that I know about my grandfather, of course, is influenced inescapably by the fact of his death. That the things I know exist almost solely in the form of symbol and color may be due to their nature in themselves; it may be equally the result, I am quite certain, of my having come to know them almost entirely through the mind and eyes, and through the shaping and desiring memory, of my mother.

The third of my grandparents' four children, my mother was born in Three Islands in 1922, in the square white house by the canal that later and for a brief time was to become a boarding-house. By the time my mother had grown old enough to form memories that would remain with her for life, my grandfather had stopped working as a brakeman on the westward-bound trains and had taken up regular shift-work in the freight and switching yards in Three Islands.

From this period—from sometime near 1925 until the sum-mer of 1938—comes my most immediate knowledge of my

grandfather. Lying within this period also are the seeds of inti-
mations that would later suggest to me something of the nature
and extent of my mother's love for her father: an infatuation
that was to shape her life and that, through her life, would alter
and influence my own in ways that I did not begin to understand for many years and that even now, after my mother's own
death, I still do not believe myself fully able to understand, or
to find understandable.

V

Among the memories that date from this period and shortly
afterward, and that have come down to me through my mother,
are the following:

1. The white goose;
2. the pot of beer;
3. Christmas oysters; barrels of iced pheasants
from South Dakota; red apples;
4. roses, hyacinths, chrysanthemums,
sunflowers, morning glories, peonies, lilacs,
lilies of the valley, bluebells,
jack-in-the-pulpits, blood root;
5. the back porch, and its changing character
and uses in summer and winter;
6. the kitchen drawer;
7. the story of the keepers of the Black Forest;
8. nicknames given to my mother by her father;
9. the wooden cabinet radio standing in a
corner of the living room;

10. whiskey;

11. classical music;

12. the violin;

13. unmade beds in upstairs bedrooms, and admonitory threats against those whose beds they were;

14. the behavior of Calvin and Victor;

15. automobiles;

16. window shades drawn against the summer heat;

17. the loss, in 1936, of my grandfather's job with the railroad;

18. a pair of knickers and a tweed cap;

19. the shape and character themselves of the square white house, with its particular placement of rooms, windows, and doors;

20. the back yard;

21. willow trees growing in the back yard along the bank of the canal;

22. the cool of summer evenings near dark;

23. the well-used footpath along the side of the canal;

24. the presence of the canal itself;

25. bed sheets hanging thickly on lines behind the house;

26. this relationship: the street running in front of the house, the canal running in back.

VI

A Notebook of My Mother

Here are some of the means by which I have become able to imagine the nature of my mother's life in the years before I was born:

1) *Pet names that have come down to me.*
Among the nicknames given by my enamored grandfather to his first daughter were the following: Red, Snip, Sparky, Stoker, Stardust, Shorty, Angel, and Sunshine. What strikes me most remarkably about these names, as I imagine back through the many years that have passed, is the way in which they seem unvaryingly to be colored now by something distant, archaic, and old-fashioned.

2) *My grandfather's infatuation.*
I believe it happened in this way: My grandfather's infatuation with his elder daughter and the many small indulgences he offered her (though, as disciplinarian and father, he made normal and conventional efforts to be fair) came about gradually through his response to my mother's alertness, her precocious responsiveness, her flirtatiousness and childhood beauty, and also through his response (as she grew older) to a greatly influential, highly treasured, and privately shared meeting of spirits that seemed later to have existed between them almost from the beginning.

3) *Idealism.*
Its way of residing communally in the heart of father and daughter, for these formative and dominant reasons: that both

were ambitious and relentlessly stubborn dreamers of reaching higher things; that both were implicit and staunch believers in the robust dignity, social respectability, and vital strength of their unrecorded blood origins; that both were unremitting idealists subject to the magnetic pull of an undefined but enthralling belief in a destined life somewhere in the future that would, in its inevitable and finally achieved form, bring to their daily existence not only privilege, wealth, and prestige, but a radiance, ease, dignity, and idealized perfection more easily imagined through color, symbol, atmosphere, and mood than expressed (for the convenience, for example, of imperceptive others) through the more concrete and homely recitation of fact or detail.

4) *Family.*

I know that these characteristics of high, allusive dreaming and of imaginative flamboyance within my grandfather were not shared readily or naturally by other members of his family. Welling up in this indefatigable and robustly dreaming man— with his muscular forearms, his sun-roughened face, and his Old World–released desire to seize the whole of a continent in his laughing embrace—were poetic visions of a subtlety and allure that were capable of striking few sympathetic or understanding notes, for example, in the limited imagination of his willingly devoted but stalwart and slow-moving wife. His two sons, from their early years, grew up hardened, unruly, sullen, and recalcitrant, as if some inexplicable strain existed in them that was foreign to any influence provided through their father, who, in the years shortly preceding his death, to a large extent fell into despair about these young men and considered them lost. His youngest child and second daughter, Leonora, was a tractable, quiet, pretty girl who seemed to live almost privately within the rest of the family, distancing herself from the rough uncertainties of her brothers' behavior and responding to her father's more zealous outward life with a modesty and caution that led him to mistake her as being less intelligent than his other children.

5) *My grandfather's third child.*

In my mother, his third child, however, was a spark that he recognized at once as being from the same flame that glowed within himself; and, in spite of his awareness that there were reasons urging the wisdom of his doing otherwise, he courted this chosen daughter. With words, laughter, small indulgences, and with a thousand harmless and increasingly habitual intimacies of kinship and spirit, he fanned the spark of her native, willing, and youth-enchanted idealism until it burst into light with a respondent eagerness and brightness that he could not possibly ever have anticipated—a brightness that survived even his own premature death not by becoming weakened or dimmed through grief but instead, more faithful than ever to the lost source of its first energy, by growing inward, adamantine, determined, secretive, and cunning: a brightness that survived faithfully even longer than that, until the time of this first daughter's own long-postponed death four decades later, although by that time, through protracted despair and through the loss not only of the future that her father had represented and embodied, but also of the past that he had been, it had grown pitiable, atrophied, confused, destructive, and diseased.

(Decades later, living in our own house in Three Islands, I

would feel at certain periods that time itself had been bent, slowed, at last stopped altogether by the enormity and strength of my mother's ruined desire. Somewhere before my own birth, I knew that time had existed in rooms, in spacious and splendid chambers: from these abandoned rooms, now sealed, locked, airless and depleted, I struggled blindly to draw breath into my own being. I sometimes, at such moments, imagined that I actually saw into the past: a high, domed, receding chamber filled with a hazy and shimmering brightness of light through which, no matter how hard I looked, I knew only that something descended toward me, stirring and shifting gently as it came nearer and nearer, lighter than dust, whispering with the emptiness of snow.)

VII

The White Goose

When they were boys, Victor and Calvin once raised a white goose in the back yard. Proving to be mean-tempered, the goose fell into the habit, when the boys allowed it to come out of its pen, of chasing my mother and her sister Leonora. When this happened, my mother and Leonora would flee in terror across the yard, seeking refuge behind the door of the back porch. Afterward, armed with long sticks, the boys in turn would chase the goose, heading it off in one direction after another, until they were able to capture it and replace it in its pen.

When the goose was grown, and after it had been allowed to frighten the girls one time too many, my grandfather one evening hung it by its feet from the branch of a willow along the canal and cut off its head with a large knife from the kitchen. After the goose was plucked, a circle of feathers lay on the grass under the willow. Smaller feathers and tufts of goose-down, having been caught by a breeze, drifted slowly away on the smooth dark water of the canal.

At the time this happened, in 1928 or 1929, my mother was six or seven years old. I did not exist, and I am unable to see these events except distantly and in tiny pieces. The two brothers, I know, wear knickers and cloth caps as I see them wielding their sticks, attempting to recapture the goose. As for the girls, however, I glimpse them even more briefly, for a fleeting moment as they move across a narrow opening in time. I see their dresses flying out as they run across the yard toward the porch. The white goose follows behind them, its long neck stretched forward.

VIII

The Pot of Beer

My mother claimed that in his early youth, before his marriage, my grandfather had mastered the violin. She believed that in learning to play the instrument he had drawn upon a gift that came down to him from an early and now untraceable source in his family heritage.

I have always secretly believed this story to be untrue, although it is in keeping with my grandfather's well-known fondness for what were considered to be beautiful things. But it seems to me just as unlikely a story, nevertheless, as another of my mother's favorite and unfounded claims about the origins of her family, namely that until the end of the eighteenth century her father's ancestors had been hereditary keepers of the Black Forest under service to the princes of the upper Rhine, and that they had thus been huntsmen and woodsmen who lived in royal dress.

I believe both of these to be stories that my grandfather invented, in my mother's early childhood, as a means of enchanting and pleasing his favorite daughter, whose imagination thrilled to the music of grandeur and color.

During the years when he worked in the switching yards, my grandfather put aside time to care assiduously for the plants and flowers outdoors around the house and yard. These were considered to be solely in my grandfather's domain, and only seldom did other members of the family help in the tending of them. Through my grandfather's efforts, morning glories climbed on strings and trellises outside the windows of the back porch, and hollyhocks and sunflowers stood each year at the side of the garage. Peony bushes and lilacs grew in the narrow front yard along the sidewalk. Roses flanked the front door, and along one side of the house was a bed of lilies of the valley, chrysanthemums, and narcissus. My grandfather was solicitous of the violets that grew near the canal in springtime, and he put wire mesh around a shaded patch of ground that produced jack-in-the-pulpit, a variety of ferns, trefoil, and blood root.

Victor and Calvin were not predisposed to be tolerant of their father's gardening or of his interest in refined things generally, and, as they grew older, they became more reckless and self-confident in their expressions of scorn for these aspects of their father's life.

My grandfather was in the habit, on Saturday nights, of listening to the symphony that was broadcast on the radio. In hot summer weather, he often carried the big radio out to the back porch and listened to the music there, in the shadowy darkness of the morning glory vines that hung on their trellises outside the screens.

On such a night, he once sent the boys to bring him a pot of beer from a tavern some blocks away. My mother, who in many ways was fondly admiring of her rough and troublesome older brothers, went along with them. On the way back from the tavern, succumbing to the temptation to show off in front of their sister, the boys drank half of the beer. Of course they could not take the pot to their father half empty, but neither did they have any money to get it filled again. Their solution to this problem was to urinate into the container and return it to their father that way.

Seldom do I know the endings of stories—whether because they are in fact unknown, or because they are the least important thing, or just because they are naturally the first part to be lost. In any case, in this story, I don't know what happened in the end. I don't know whether my mother, caught between fidelity to her brothers and fidelity to her father, ran ahead in the darkness to warn him of the truth, or whether she stood by in pained uncertainty, watching him take the first drink as music from the radio filled the night air of the screened porch. I don't know whether fury and violence followed, or in what forms; whether the boys stayed home; or whether they fled into the night.

My mother was ten years old at the time of this story, which took place in 1932. The ending, of course, would have made no difference in any case. But I continue to think of another, more significant, moment: I imagine the three children stopping on their way back from the tavern to confer together in shadowy darkness under trees, a streetlight shining steadily nearby; and the boys, their shoulders pressed together, conspiratorially turning their backs on their sister.

IX

The house they lived in was unshaded by trees, since these were small and sparse in the immediate vicinity and, except for the willows at the bank of the canal, grew only along one edge of the lot. This openness gave the house a raw, stark, unprotected appearance which my grandfather's flowers, when they were in bloom, had the odd effect of heightening rather than diminishing. The front yard was little more than eight or ten feet deep, and there was no front porch other than a roofed-over stoop just large enough for a single chair to be placed at either side of the door. In the back yard, stretched between prominent T-shaped wooden poles, hung clotheslines.

In summer, the sun beat down on the house without remorse; in hottest weather, against the heat of the day, my grandmother drew yellow-brown shades in all of the windows, upstairs and down.

Along the bank of the canal was a well-worn footpath, where my grandfather was especially fond of strolling in the summer evenings after dinner. During a certain part of her later childhood, my mother fell into the habit of going with him, and often they strolled a mile or more before turning back, to the point at the edge of town where the canal made a wide slow curve on its path westward across the plains toward Joliet. Darkness often fell before their return. Children were called in from yards and streets. Lights came on in the upstairs windows of houses they passed. Sometimes mist lifted up from the unmoving water of the canal, rising in thin reeds and wisps like smoke. The grass they walked on would be wet with dew when they came across the back yard to the door of the porch, where a light would be shining inside the kitchen window.

.

At Christmas, in part because of my grandfather's work in the switching yards, the fruits of the nation's wealth would come to the family, arriving by way of the far-flung railroad lines that converged upon the town from across the continent. Each year, from the freight yard, my grandfather would bring home a wooden barrel with oysters packed in ice that had been sent by rail from New Orleans, and another, of unplucked pheasants, that had arrived from the distant farm in South Dakota where my great-aunt Bethany lived. A third barrel, of hard red apples, would come from Wisconsin, where another of my grandmother's sisters lived. For each of three consecutive nights after work, my grandfather would bring home one of the barrels, carrying it balanced on his shoulder as he walked from the trolley stop. He would pass under a streetlight, move for a time through darkness, then pass under another light, making his way home.

.

When he lost his job with the bankrupt railroad in 1936, my grandfather, in an effort to keep money of some kind coming into the household, suppressed his pride and took up work as a golf caddy. In good weather from spring through fall, he would leave the house in the morning and go by trolley to the passenger station in Three Islands. By local train, he would travel to the suburbs south of Chicago, or sometimes to the far north side, and hitchhike or walk to one of the golf courses, where he would spend the day working for tips. He was strong, patient, and quietly good-humored with the golfers, who, as they gradually came to know his reputation for these qualities, increasingly sought out his services.

His dress consisted of knickers and a white shirt and tweed cap—items of clothing that my mother in particular found sharply humiliating and inappropriate to my grandfather's rightful station in life, but that my grandfather himself made small and encouraging jokes about, declaring with a jaunty but perhaps false confidence that he would find more respectable work before long or that the railroad would reorganize and would soon begin rehiring.

Calvin by this time was eighteen years old, but he found himself able to get work only sporadically and for short periods of time as a delivery boy or, very occasionally, as a carpenter's helper. A year and a half younger than his brother, Victor had quietly dropped out of school. Leonora had reached her twelfth birthday.

The two brothers continued to live at home during this time, although they were now charged a weekly fee of two dollars each for their room and board. If their beds went unmade or their room was disorderly, they were expected to pay a fine of fifteen cents, a requirement more likely to be honored by Calvin than by Victor. More and more often, Victor failed to return home at night altogether, remaining uninclined to disclose his whereabouts.

.

During this difficult and uncertain period in the history of her family, my mother was observed, for the first time in her life, to display a temperament that was uncommunicative, subdued, and withdrawn, and to behave in ways that were often dramatically unpredictable as to temper and mood. She had reached an age, of course, at which changes of this kind can be considered a normal aspect of the difficult passage out of girlhood into womanhood and, as such, might have been allowed to pass as unremarkable. In the case of my mother, however, I cannot help but think that the change possessed an additional and inward significance: I imagine that my mother, for the first time in her life, had begun to perceive that time itself could not be trusted; that there was no guarantee of its carrying her forward into an ideal future; that the necessity might arise for her, surrounded by ruins, to pursue her life alone, grappling with enemies.

.

My mother was doomed. Therefore I was doomed with her.

TRAVEL

My father's paternal grandfather, in 1859, emigrated at age fourteen from what then was the kingdom of Prussia, traveled thousands of miles, and settled on a farm in the bottomlands along the lower Missouri River. My father himself, in 1939, made a journey of three hundred miles when he came to Three Islands from the town of Ambrose, Missouri, where he had grown up. Not long after they were married, my mother traveled only five blocks, the distance from her childhood home to our own house in Three Islands.

It seemed clear to me that the journeys taken by members of our family were growing shorter and that in keeping with this pattern my own journeys would by necessity be shorter still. I could, of course, walk from the front steps of our house to the bank of the canal, and from there to the candy and tobacco store a block and a half in the opposite direction. Or I might go to Pederson's corner grocery and, coming home by way of the path that cut through the interior of our own block, return to the back door of our house. My travels might in equal likelihood take place within the confines and privacy of my room itself, where I could travel in whatever way I wished: from the door to my bed; from the bed to my desk; from my desk to the window, where, through trees, I could see the canal.

·

I sometimes imagined history as a sworl, an enormous, cloud-trailing funnel larger than the earth, rotating with a grand, opaque, majestic slowness and tapering gradually to a single point, where, as if through the briefly opened lens of a camera, a single moment and place in time would be revealed, then blinked out once again and obscured. I sometimes imagined this great, slowly rotating cyclone shaping itself with a cosmic slowness to its single point and then opening its shutter for the most fleeting of moments on my own place and my own time: on the homely town of Three Islands, Illinois, with its flat streets and empty sidewalks; on our house, its wooden clapboards painted white, standing on its street by the canal; and on me, sitting on the front steps, wearing shorts and a T-shirt on an August afternoon in 1955, waiting patiently for the hushed, still, motionless, heat-oppressed and green-shadowed depth of the summer afternoon to give way gradually to the changing light and whispered coolness of evening.

·

The truth was that escape had become impossible for any of us, of course, now that history had stopped entirely, having slipped away one summer morning, with a brief glint of sunlight on the side of a turning car, through an invisible opening in green foliage at the far end of our street.

.

Looking back, I think of our lives in those years as having taken place in silence, or perhaps only amid sounds that I am unable to hear. Even the most difficult periods of my mother's illness, falling often near the anniversaries and marking-places of death, seem to me now to have occurred wordlessly, and to remain suspended somehow in a timeless and curiously slow-motioned mime: when, near my seventeenth birthday, my mother ran after my grandmother through the downstairs rooms of our house with a carving knife, until my grandmother escaped out the front door; or, near the same impossible and despairing time, when she came into my room with the kitchen shears and, opening my dresser and closet, flung my clothing out into the air, an event that seems to me now to have occurred a thousand years ago, unmoved and drifting in time: I imagine my clothing—skirts, blouses, jumpers, sweaters, shoes— fluttering in the air of my room, suspended gently near the ceiling on softly stirring currents, turning weightlessly there like a thick and colorful snow.

.

Across the street from us lived an obese girl named Rebecca Bronson, who spent entire afternoons sitting on her porch swing. Carlotta Tepp and I, and sometimes my brother Julian, would ask for pennies from our mothers. For each penny, Rebecca would perform, successfully touching the tip of her nose with her tongue. After she had done this, not having moved from her swing, we would sometimes sit on the steps of her porch and talk, waiting for a part of the afternoon to pass by.

When I was eight years old, my mother made a layer cake

for me, its white icing decorated to reveal the face of a clock, its ornate red hands, because of my age, pointing precisely to the hour of eight. The cake was a success and a great curiosity among the gathering of my friends who had come to help me celebrate. Only many years later, when I was a student at the College of West Tree, did I understand why I had come to find the memory of it terrifying, although I still did not know at what point this had begun to be the case.

·

My brother Julian rode his tricycle unceasingly up and down the sidewalk in front of our house. He pedaled to the bank of the canal, came back and went past the house as far as the first street corner, then returned to the canal, and again rode back, in a circular journey that came to an end only when he was called in for supper, or for bed. He once, slightly older, spent a day painting the weathered-gray boards and steps of the back porch with a paintbrush and bucket of water. As they dried and turned pale, he would return again and again, moistening the old boards into an illusion of freshness.

·

When he came home from work each night, my father would pause on the back porch to unlace and take off his boots. Inside the kitchen door each day was a fresh square of newspaper. My father would set his work boots on it, side by side, placing them in the center of the newspaper, precisely parallel with the edges of the sheet.

·

On wash days, my mother worked quickly, with a grim determination and often with an unhappy fierceness of mood. In the back yard, our clothes would hang on lines as if we ourselves were exposed there, strewn in disarray, unanchored in time and space. Headless or armless, with empty legs or footless, we hung upside down, or sideways, or right side up in a spectacle of disorder, dismemberment, and madness, the empty and dislocated pieces of us—my grandmother's empty print dresses, my father's work pants and shirts, varieties of mournfully isolated socks and pieces of absurdly large and small underwear, the flared cotton skirts my mother wore—a kaleidoscope of broken pieces touched into vestigial twitches of movement by passing breezes or, on windy days, flapping like a ludicrous gathering of the damned, raising, without voices, a chorus of discomfiture and lamentation.

.

One early evening during a week's vacation in Wisconsin, my mother and grandmother stayed on shore while my father took Julian and me onto the lake to fish. Far out in the middle of the lake, we left our lines in the water almost until dark, when, at the time to return, my father found that the motor would not start. Darkness fell around us as he pulled at the rope, took off the cover of the motor, replaced it, pulled again at the rope. A breeze caused us to drift farther across the lake. There was no moon. My father changed places with Julian and me, set the oars into the locks and rowed us back slowly through the darkness in the direction of our cabin. Tiny waves slapped against the boat, and Julian fell asleep, leaning against me on our seat in the back. My mother and my grandmother waited together at the end of the dock with a lantern. When we came near, my mother held the lantern out over the water; I remember how it illuminated their two faces, bent together in the surrounding darkness, looking down at us steadily from above as the boat touched against the piles of the dock.

1938

I

In my mind's eye, I have seen my grandfather's death a thousand times. The story of it comes to me in briefly glimpsed fragments that are accompanied by shadow and light and by a certain number of heightened, vivid colors.

.

Unvaryingly, I first see my mother and grandmother walking to the hospital in Three Islands. For reasons that I do not wholly understand, I watch them from above, as if I were floating a certain distance over the treetops, looking down at them.

My mother wears a white dress, my grandmother a blue one. The date is August 23rd, 1938. The afternoon sky is cloudless and deep; the summer air is still. My mother and my grandmother are obscured frequently from my view as they walk beneath the foliage of trees, but I see them clearly when they emerge at the end of each block, walking side by side, then enter another tunnel of what I imagine to be cool and sundappled shade.

Two weeks before this moment, my grandfather went into the hospital to have his appendix removed. Although he has lost weight, he is believed now to have recovered from the operation and is to return home. Dressed in his street clothes, which are now baggy and loose on him, he sits on a chair beside the window in his hospital room, waiting for the arrival of my grandmother and my mother. My mother at this time is only a week away from her seventeenth birthday. She is pretty and remarkably youthful and slender; she wears her dark hair pinned back behind her ears, from where it falls down loosely almost to her shoulders.

.

From my place above the tops of the trees, I see my grandmother and my mother go up the walkway and into the main entrance of the hospital, the blue dress and then the white one disappearing through the revolving door.

.

I see them next from inside the hospital, where they are standing at my grandfather's door as if about to enter his room. The door has been left slightly ajar. My grandmother stands back for a moment, and at the same time my mother leans tentatively forward; her hand touches the door just above its handle, and her posture suggests that she is about to peer into the room, pushing the door farther open if necessary, as if to ascertain whether my grandfather is asleep or awake.

The room is on the third and top story of the hospital, and the corridor there is spacious, wide, and very nearly empty. At each end of the corridor stands a high window that rises from near the floor up almost to the ceiling, where it terminates in a fan-shaped arch. Daylight from each of these windows falls across the polished floor but does not reach far enough to dispel the shadowy darkness gathered at the center point of the corridor. Various glass panes in each window are tilted open, and through the corridor moves a soft current of cool fresh air.

My mother and my grandmother are not alone in the corridor. At its midpoint, in the gathered half-darkness there, a nurse sits at a wooden table placed against one wall. A shaded lamp casts a light across sheets of paper arranged before her. The nurse is dressed in white; she wears a cap that rises crest-like above her forehead. Holding her pen just over the surface of a piece of paper, she turns to look down the hall toward my mother and my grandmother; she continues to watch them standing at the doorway to my grandfather's room, as if she, too, is waiting to discover whether my grandfather is asleep or awake.

.

My mother opens the door only for a moment, and then not fully; it takes my mother and my grandmother only a second or two to disappear inside and then to push the door almost closed again behind them.

The fleeting glimpse that I am allowed to see of the interior of the room is like a certain kind of painting from the early part of the century—I think of Matisse, for example—that I might see hanging in a museum.

The interior of the room appears to be filled with a shadowy, cool, pleasant half-darkness. In the momentary and restricted view I have, I see only parts of things, but the parts I do see are remarkably vivid in the soft darkness from which they seem to emerge, or within which they seem to be suspended. I am able, for example, to see a part of the foot of the bed: the curve of the iron bedstead is painted a thick, creamy white; a blanket is folded neatly at the foot of the mattress. Part of the chair is

visible in which my grandfather sits as he waits for my mother
and my grandmother to arrive. Of my grandfather himself, I
can see a knee, one forearm, a hand. Beside the chair in which
he sits, part of the open window is visible. Thick green foliage
presses up against it, brightened by afternoon sunlight.

.

My grandfather's death occurred when a blood clot, having
traveled for some time undetected inside his body, entered his
heart and remained there, causing it to stop beating. I do not,
for whatever reason, see the precise moment of his death.

From the hallway outside the room, I can neither see nor
hear what happens inside. I do not see, for example, the expression on my grandfather's face as the door at last opens
inward; I do not hear the characteristic, familiar joke he makes
about the probable reasons for the lateness of my mother and
my grandmother's arrival. I do not see him push himself up
carefully from the chair, declaring as he does so that he believes
himself fit and ready to go back to work, and that it is beyond
his understanding why he has been kept in the hospital even for
this long. I do not see him step from the window toward my
mother, who, at the same time, moves toward her father. And I
do not see him come to a stop as his face turns suddenly blank;
then, looking past my mother toward something else, becomes
deeply puzzled; then, almost as suddenly, is overcome by what
appears to be pain and uncomprehending terror. I see nothing
as he begins to fall, first to his knees, then to the floor, where,
in the presence of my mother and my grandmother, he lies with
one arm curled under his chest, the other reaching out.

All of this takes place for me in a distant and absolute silence,
as if an invisible heavenful of cotton had descended to fill up

the atmosphere around me. But it is clear to me, nevertheless, that a certain number of sounds have been made—screams, perhaps; the calling out of my grandfather's name; cries for help. I know this (from wherever it is that I really am, wherever it is in fact that I am watching from) because I know that the nurse leaps up suddenly from her writing table, and with her white dress flying out behind her, runs with great haste along the corridor toward the door of my grandfather's room.

II

Leonora was at home at the time of the death, having been left in charge of preparing a pork roast and browned potatoes, a meal chosen for that particular afternoon as being her father's favorite. The hospital telephoned her almost immediately, and she in turn summoned a neighbor who went to the place where Calvin was then working; within half an hour, Calvin arrived at the hospital (Leonora, making her way on foot, had preceded him) to give what comfort he could to his mother and sisters, and later to escort them home. Victor's whereabouts were unknown, and not until twelve hours later, in a tavern on First Street whose front door had been locked for some time but whose back door remained open, was he to hear the news by chance. Much earlier that day, in the forenoon of August 23rd, before my mother and grandmother walked to the hospital in their white and blue dresses, a large washing had been done. At the moment of my grandfather's death, white sheets and various articles of clothing hung on lines in the back yard to dry.

I think of my grandfather's death as the central event in my mother's life, as a single and irreversible moment of absence and loss that became for her at once a dividing moment in time.

I do not know if it is true that my mother was changed by my grandfather's death. I know that I believe it to be so. It has become impossible for me not to think of my mother's earlier life as leading up to the moment of my grandfather's death, and impossible for me not to think of her subsequent life—including her life of marriage and having children—as leading backward to it.

·

When my mother was eleven years old and Leonora nine—in 1933—the two sisters spent a part of the summer on the farm in South Dakota where their aunt Bethany lived with her husband, a man unrelated to them but known as their uncle Paul. For a certain number of years following, they made this trip again, staying on the farm for four or five weeks each summer.

Their return home each year was by train, and an image of them on this journey has remained in my mind from almost as far back in my childhood as I am able to remember.

After it picked them up in South Dakota, the train took them across southern Minnesota, went over the Mississippi River, briefly touched a corner of Wisconsin, then continued southward through Illinois to Three Islands. When I see them, they are invariably somewhere in the far southwestern part of Minnesota. Outside the windows of the train extends what appears to be a limitless prairie of gently rolling hills covered with high grass that under the sun of late summer has become a tawny gold, revealing the remaining pale green of its undersides only occasionally when a passing wind ruffles or parts it. In this image, I see my mother and my aunt Leonora from inside the railroad car, which is old-fashioned in style, with square windows that are opened by sliding the panes downward from the top. I am near the back of the car, and I see the two sisters from behind, watching them where they sit, side by side, halfway toward the front. The rest of the car is empty. The girls are young and small, and they sit primly, looking straight ahead. They wear flat-brimmed hats made of plaited straw, and a ribbon is tied with a bow around each crown, one of them red and the other yellow. With the swaying motion of the train, their heads move slightly from side to side, in unison.

When I see them, the train is going around a wide curve on the prairie, and, through the windows on the left side of the car, the entire length of the train is visible for a time, including the engine, far off in the distance, leaving a thin trail of smoke behind as it draws them swiftly toward home.

·

In a dream, from extremely close up, I see the engineer's cocked elbow and the top of his striped cap as the engine of a train plunges suddenly past me, in silence. Then I find myself somewhere in the near distance, watching the train speed westward under a sky that looks soft and gold, as if the sun, descending toward the horizon, were penetrating through high sheets of falling rain. The young grass of the prairie is not yet tall, and, to the edges of the earth all around, it is sprinkled with small blue and white flowers. On top of the rushing caboose I see my grandfather, sitting on a kitchen chair, playing the violin. His sleeves are rolled to the elbows and a railroad cap is perched on his head, its visor pointing jauntily upward. I can see his bow arm moving back and forth, and, as the train draws him closer to me, I watch him raise his face toward the golden sky in an expression of near-anguished pleasure at the beauties of the instrument's phrasings. But then the train carries him quickly past me, and, playing a music I cannot hear, he is swept away westward into the unbroken and profound silence that presses in everywhere around me, until the caboose he rides on diminishes to a tiny point on the far distant edge of the horizon, remains poised there for a moment, then disappears entirely from my view.

ARRIVALS

I

i

Money. My grandfather's death left his family in a pressing financial position that threatened to allow their lives to fall into squalor. His own income for the previous two years had been sporadic and often inconsequential; after his death, what savings there may once have been were depleted. Calvin continued to draw in money, although irregularly and most often in extremely small amounts. From time to time Victor also contributed to the family's expenses, but just as frequently, in the months after his father's death, he fell into the habit of removing certain amounts of money from the wooden drawer in the kitchen where current household bills and the grocery funds were kept and using them for purposes about which he remained unforthcoming, secretive, and devious.

In September, instead of returning to high school for her

senior year, my mother applied for work at the telephone company, where, after training, she was given a position as night operator. At the same time, my grandmother began the task of converting the square white house into a boardinghouse for men who had come to the area to find jobs in the new oil refinery outside of Three Islands.

Rooms. Calvin and Victor kept their own room as before; my mother, my aunt Leonora, and my grandmother, however, moved together into the adjacent corner bedroom in the rear. This allowed space for two lodgers in the large front bedroom and another in what had been Leonora's small side room. Downstairs, the dining room was converted also into a room for two lodgers. The living room, with the dining table moved into it, came to be used as a place for meals, although three or four pieces of living room furniture remained, pushed back against the walls, so that the room functioned also as a parlor or lounge. My grandfather's cabinet radio continued to stand in one corner, where it had stood before. In the evenings, men sat in chairs and listened to it, some of them reading the newspaper. Others sat at the table playing games of cards.

Hours. Leonora stayed in school after her father's death, but she got up two hours earlier than usual each morning to help with breakfast and with preparation of the lodgers' box lunches. My mother's shift at the telephone company ended at six o'clock in the morning, at which time she would also return home and, after Leonora had gone off to school, help my grandmother with making beds, doing laundry, and cleaning the house for an hour or two before going to bed herself at nine or ten o'clock. When she woke up late in the afternoon, she had time to help with the preparation and serving of the evening meal, then, before returning to the telephone company at ten P.M., to lend a hand in clearing up the kitchen and laying things out for the following day. Only on Sundays did the schedule vary greatly, since on that day there were no box lunches to be prepared, and the evening meal was not served.

Sleep. During the time when my mother slept, the house was often entirely empty, since the lodgers were at work, Leonora was at school, and my grandmother commonly used the middle hours of the day for shopping and for visits to the houses of relatives and friends. The boardinghouse, at these times, would surround my sleeping mother in a state of careful and fastidious preparation. The lodgers' rooms would be clean and their beds neatly made, pairs of shoes placed side by side on the floor, folded towels and washcloths hung on rods fixed to closet doors. At the table in the living room, places would already be set for the evening meal. Knives and forks, waiting for absent hands to grasp them, would rest patiently beside empty glasses and plates. The kitchen itself would be vacant and silent. Invariably, in good weather, the door to the back porch would be set open to let in the afternoon air.

ii

My father came from Missouri to Three Islands in the summer of 1939 with 450 dollars in savings, a two-year-old Chevrolet, and a letter agreeing to give him a job as treater in the refinery outside of town.

He was twenty-two years old at this time. For the first several weeks that he worked at the refinery, he lived in a second-floor room over Jarchow's grocery at Third Street and Central Avenue. It was a living place, however, that from the beginning he thought of as temporary, since the owners of the rooms offered neither laundry services nor board.

One night in a tavern two blocks from his room and a block and a half down First Street toward the canal, he met Victor. After they had talked for a time, and after my father had bought him one or two drinks, Victor mentioned the boardinghouse that his mother maintained. He had not been there himself for the past two or three days, he explained. But the last he'd been aware, he thought there had been a vacancy in the house.

.

My father, on a still afternoon in July, went up to the front door of the square white house on the canal to inquire about lodgings. I have heard about this moment innumerable times; and I have come, over the many passing years, to imagine it as the moment, out of nothingness, when my own being was first unknowingly and blindly summoned toward existence.

The front door of the house is closed, and yellowed shades are drawn in all the windows. After glancing once up toward the roof and the upstairs windows, my father goes up the short walkway, climbs the three steps, pauses briefly, and knocks at the door. He is dressed in an open white shirt and workman's dark trousers.

Behind him on the otherwise empty street, the car that he drove in from Missouri stands in the sun, its wheels turned toward the curb. As he stands at the door listening for a response, the afternoon around him seems immense and endless in its quietness. There are no sounds at all except, now and again, in brief choruses, the lazily rising and falling cries of cicadas. No one else, as my father knocks at the door once again, and then again, seems to be nearby, anywhere.

.

My mother, fast asleep at the back of the house, heard nothing at first. Then a sound reached her as if from within a dream, half waking her. Repeated yet again, it came from downstairs like something distant, muted, off-stage: the faraway sound of my father's knocking in the poised, hushed, vacant, afternoon silence of the empty house.

.

My father's first sight of her—this slender, pretty, dark-haired, dark-eyed girl—was a sight of her in the quiet flush of impatience and irritation. With one hand, she held the door open just far enough for them to look one another up and down. With the other, she firmly clasped the front of the robe she wore.

.

Her reply to my father's inquiry was that she could tell him nothing about a vacancy, but that he was free to wait on the steps, or on one of the chairs by the door, for her mother to return to the house.

He did this, sitting for an hour on the steps in front of the closed door, then for an hour and a half, then somewhat longer. Shadows began very slightly to lengthen. His car stood motionless on the street. At last, on the sidewalk at the far end of the block, appeared my grandmother. In a dark print dress, wearing a hat with a pearl-tipped pin in it, her shoulders sagging from the weight of the shopping bags that hung down from each hand, she made her way slowly toward the young man waiting on her step.

II

i
The Other Man

I was ten or eleven years old, in 1951 or 1952, when my mother went back for a time to her job at the telephone company, before she found better-paying work in the Loop and began to take the train into the city each morning.

She began on a split shift, finishing work at ten o'clock in the evening, and I sometimes went along with my father to pick her up in the car. I was fond of these trips, sitting in the car with my father outside the old telephone building downtown, under a street light, with no one around us on the empty sidewalks or the deserted street.

When my mother came out through the side door of the building, it was often possible to predict her mood—by the way she paused just outside the closed door, for example, and, after fumbling through her purse, impatiently struck a match to light a cigarette, or by the sharpness and quickness of her step as she came toward us, not looking up.

I would climb into the back seat, and if my mother's temper was bad (I could sometimes tell by how hard she slammed the door), there would be a tense uneasiness as my father drove us home, with unsuccessful, awkward, and desultory attempts at conversation.

But just as often my mother would wait until she was settled comfortably in the front seat of the car before lighting a cigarette, and there would be an easy flow of talk as she asked questions of us, or offered up bits of gossip from her shift, or told about the latest new development in the life of one of the women she worked with.

At these times, my father drove slowly, with a relaxed and cautiously expansive air, his bent elbow resting on the ledge of his open window. Occasionally, he would turn up onto Central Avenue, park the car and go into Doppelmann's drug store, then come out with three ice cream cones. We drove home as we were still eating them, and my mother, without being asked, would sometimes reach over and hold the steering wheel for my father when he needed an extra hand to shift gears. This seemed to me an eloquently simple and intimate gesture, and at such moments, from my place in the back seat, I imagined that I was seeing a glimpse of my parents from years earlier, in the brief time when they met and were first married, before they lived in the house we now lived in, and before I had come into their lives.

For a week or two during that summer, my mother altered her schedule, taking on an additional part of a night shift in order to help cover for a woman who had had a death in her family. The telephone company at that time was still in its old building, three blocks off Central Avenue, where First Street came to an end alongside the canal. The switchboard was on the basement floor at the rear, toward the water, and my mother told us that during the early morning hours when she was alone at the switchboard, a man would come to the screen door and talk with her.

The first night he appeared, he explained to her the story of his life—about how he had become an orphan, how he had wandered for many years as a vagrant, riding freight cars from one side of the continent to the other, working for different periods of time wherever he was able to find work. On following nights, my mother would unlatch the screen door and fill a cup for him from her thermos of coffee; then she would latch the door again, fill her own cup, and they would drink their coffee together on the two sides of the screen as she listened to his stories and told him her own, the long ramble of their conversation interrupted only by calls that came through the switchboard at infrequent and sporadic intervals, placed by those few others who were also awake in the sleeping town.

My mother came off her segment of the shift at four o'clock in the morning, and my father would get out of bed to go meet her, leaving the rest of us asleep in the house. I did not go with him, of course, and so did not immediately hear my mother tell her story. Hearing it later, however, I had reason once more to wonder, as I had had before and would again, whether any part of it was really the truth. As for my father, as was his custom, he said nothing in my hearing, and not, so far as I know, in hers, that might suggest his own doubt and that might be interpreted therefore as a betrayal of my mother. For my own part, however true or untrue the story itself of the man at the door may have been, I have always found within it something pitiable and memorable and fleetingly dramatic. I have often imagined my father pulling up at the curb of the deserted street at the beginning of that earliest, dew-hushed hour of the summer morning; and, at precisely the moment of my father's arrival, the shadowy figure of the other man, at the rear of the building, getting to his feet and disappearing into the darkness along the canal.

ii

Doorway

On the day in the fall of 1945 when my father returned from Hawaii, my mother sent me to the house of a neighbor across the street. I was four and a half years old, and although I had seen photographs of him, I had no clear memory of my father.

The neighbor was a woman whom I thought of as extremely old and who lived alone. I disliked the stillness and the closed-in feeling of her house, although I don't specifically remember being frightened of her. I do recall being given paper and drawing materials at her kitchen table when I arrived near lunchtime, and I remember clearly the slow crawl of the seemingly endless afternoon. I stood at the woman's front window, between the long lace curtains there and the glass panes, keeping watch in order not to miss the arrival of my father. My mother was nowhere in sight. From across the street, the blank windows and closed front door of our own house gazed back at me imperturbably.

When he appeared, walking from the far end of the street, my father carried a suitcase in each hand. I watched him closely as he came nearer. On the sidewalk in front of our house he paused for a moment, glanced toward the upstairs windows and roof, then turned onto the short walkway and went up the steps to the door.

My mother, a hidden mirror image of myself, had been watching for him also: the door opened just as he reached it, and my mother put her arms around my father's neck and clung there. She wore a sleeveless dress, and I remember vividly the pale whiteness of her arms.

From across the street, I watched as my father picked up the suitcases that he had set down beside him; as my mother stepped backward, withdrawing into the darkness behind the doorway; as my father followed her; as the door was then once again closed.

iii

Sea

When I was born, in March of 1941 in the red brick hospital in Three Islands where my grandfather had died, my mother was given drugs that drew her deeply into sleep. So profoundly did she sleep that she fell away toward the distant veil of time itself and, passing through to the other side, came into a vast meadow covered as far as the eye could see with high grass and golden yellow flowers.

My mother did not speak of the veil of time, or of passing through to the other side. But when she told me this story, the many times she did so in my childhood, her voice was soft and quiet and enchanting and intimate and low.

Radiant, hushed, and soft, the meadow was the loveliest of places my mother was ever to see. The sky, half visible, loomed high overhead; a soft golden mist fell all around her, touching her shoulders and face and arms, as if light itself were falling down in quiet waves through the air. Across the meadow stood my grandfather, his arms open as if beckoning to my mother, who, in the dream, ran toward him through the yellow flowers, struggling toward him valiantly against the weight of some unearthly power that made her limbs feel leaden and that held her back with an indescribable heaviness drawing against her body.

How distant we were from one another, my mother and I, even then, at the moment of my birth: I, struggling blindly toward the surface of a turbulent and drowning sea; my mother, at the same moment, with every effort of her being, beating her way downward toward its silent, vaulted depths.

iv

Moments

(Carlotta Tepp and I and my brother Julian playing house in the attic, among the sheets and towels hanging there on lines to dry. The sound of the cold wind outdoors, the spatter of rain and sleet tossed against the panes of the single window at one end of the attic. My mother's rap at the door. Her bringing us a tray of "tea." The four of us sitting on the floor, by the rain-flung window, drinking it from warm cups.

.

The smell of autumn, sweet air, the tang of new promise. School clothes, pencils and erasers, a new three-ring notebook. My mother standing outside the front door of our house as I went to the corner and waited there for Carlotta, then watching as the two of us walked to school. The unbearable melancholy of the scent of autumn, especially in the afternoons.

.

The telephone ringing at night, in the first moments of calm after a summer storm. My father going downstairs to answer it, then getting dressed quickly and driving off to the place where a pipeline had been exposed by a washout, or where a valve or main needed to be closed because of fallen lines or a lightning

strike. In the damp, still air of morning, when I got out of bed,
twigs and leaves and small limbs would be scattered across the
wet lawns and sidewalks and streets. Sometimes a tree would
have fallen, or a big limb would be hanging down, white wood
exposed at the point where it had been wrenched away.

.

My mother's unremitting and fastidious housekeeping, the
unflagging energy she devoted to it, and the great strength of
her desire for cleanliness and order: washed windows and curtains, laundered rugs, vacuumed carpet, folded linens, clean
ashtrays, polished furniture. My father using a tall ladder on
weekends one spring to scrape and paint the outside of our
house. The particular and oddly secretive pleasantness especially of the kitchen late at night, with everything in its place or
hidden and out of sight: the room lighted only by the one small
lamp under the cupboards above the sink, or by nothing but
the faint beam from the street light through the side window.
The memory of my mother on the back porch, squatting on
her heels with a stiff brush, scrubbing at the caked earth that
clung to my father's work boots.

.

That there was another side to everything about her: like
a mirror that reflects things normally but that also, like a
window, lets you see through into a shadowy world behind
its surface: lets you see into a place, beyond time, that can't
really exist.

.

My mother's way of looking at me, during periods of difficulty or anger, as though she did not see me, or as though I
weren't even there and she was looking through me. Her say-

ing to Carlotta, once when we were in high school: I'm sure *your* mother is a good mother.

.

My understanding none of this until later. Its being by then much too late.

.

The incident of my schoolbooks, near the end of eleventh grade. My mother leaning in the doorway of the bathroom with her arms crossed over her chest while, barefoot and wearing only my nightgown, I brushed my teeth at the sink. My imagining later that my mother did not see me at all, but instead saw my reflection in the bathroom window at my side: a ghost-image of me, outside of time, suspended somewhere in the night air above our yard, bent forward over the sink, brushing my teeth. That she saw not me, but herself at my age, then despised me, because she was gone.

.

That I was ungrateful. My mother's great, unleashed anger, her accusing me afterward of ingratitude, when from the desk in my room she took my notebooks and papers and books, carried them downstairs and plunged them into the wastebasket under the sink before collapsing at the table in sobs. My father going into the room. My mother telling him, her passion unspent, that she never wanted to see me again.

.

I was a mirror. My mother wanted me broken.

.

My brother Julian, after school, going into the back yard and throwing his rubber ball high against the gabled wall of the house, then catching it when it came down. His doing this repeatedly, counting the number of times he was able to throw the ball and catch it without missing.

·

My coming to understand only so much later that my mother was helpless and already defeated, wrestling with time itself: that the countless memories I have of her, in the kitchen, for example, preparing dinner in rage, are in reality memories of her, in the kitchen, preparing dinner in despair; or what it meant one night late in autumn, after the grass had been browned by frost, when my grandmother, pursued by my mother, ran out the front door and then in a wide circle around the outside of our house; and what it was that I really saw, peering down from the window of my room, when I watched the pale white flash of my grandmother's bare feet, and when I saw her nightgown, like my own, flying out behind her in the ghostly darkness.

·

In my room, I sat at my desk reading. In the house below me, her face still young and pretty, my mother looked out first through one window and then another. On her bed above me, my grandmother gazed sightlessly at the ceiling and sky.

·

In the spring of the year, my mother and my grandmother picking asparagus in the old grass on the far bank of the canal. Bent forward, holding baskets on their arms. The breeze rippling their skirts, flaring them out to one side, pressing the thin colored fabric against their legs.)

SEEING

The first time something went wrong with my eyes was in the spring of eleventh grade. I didn't know why it happened. I kept it a secret from everyone.

.

The day was warm, gusty, and unsettled. When I walked to school with Carlotta in the morning, our skirts blew and flared around our legs in the balmy air, and the branches of trees, heavy with new green foliage, tossed and rustled over our heads.

During my next-to-last class that afternoon, a tiny knife gash appeared in the center of my vision, allowing a steadily shimmering light to come through from a vast empty space beyond. This small gash did not disappear but instead grew rapidly larger. I became unnerved; then frightened; and at last, in the grip of sudden panic, I left the room abruptly, abandoning my books and notebooks and pencils on the desk behind me.

·

I thought at first, looking up at Miss Ebertson where she stood in the front of the room, that it would be a small and momentary thing that would quickly go away. I closed my eyes and squeezed the bridge of my nose. Behind my closed eyelids, I could still see the small three-cornered opening, like a small rip in a piece of stretched silk. Its widening edges seemed to quiver, and beyond it, although reddened now by the blood of my eyelids, was only light.

By waiting, and by trying to keep my breathing slow and regular, I thought that I could make it go away. When I opened my eyes and looked at Miss Ebertson again, however, I found that I was unable to see the whole of her face at once. I was unable to see her eyes if I looked directly at them, although, doing so, I could still see her mouth, with its small gray lips speaking words to the class. But if I looked directly at her mouth, it disappeared in turn behind the quivering hole of light and I could see only Miss Ebertson's eyes and the top of her face.

Ahead of me, in the row alongside the windows, Carlotta sat half sideways in her seat, looking down idly at her desk, the side of her head supported by her raised forearm. When I closed my eyes, I saw that the shape was taking on a vaguely circular form, like the widening aperture in the lens of a camera. My breathing quickened in a sudden rush of fear, and for a fleeting moment my body seemed entirely weightless. When I looked toward Carlotta again, I could see only the tip of her elbow resting against her desk top, the rest of her having disappeared entirely into the field of shimmering white light. This was when I found myself on my feet and already fleeing from the room.

·

For a time, a narrow periphery of vision remained, and I guided myself by it, seeing things by not looking at them. I came out of a side entrance of the building and left the school behind me. I wore no jacket or sweater, but only my blue skirt and white blouse with short sleeves. As I set out across the grassless and pebbly dirt of the empty school yard toward home, the wind moved in warm freshets around my bare arms.

·

Before I got home I could no longer see with my own eyes except as if through a large window into a sea of light; and yet, for a reason that I did not then entirely understand, it seemed to me also that I was still able to observe myself, and in that way to find my path. I seemed to watch myself from above, from a vantage somewhere a certain distance over the top of the tossing spring foliage. No one else, in this view, was anywhere in sight on the warm, wind-tossed, empty streets: only me. From my vantage place above, I watched myself, in my blue skirt and white blouse, as I was obscured under the restless foliage of trees, then as I emerged, crossed an empty street, and was hidden again, until at last I reappeared and turned into our own street, made my way down our block toward the canal, cut across the small strip of our front lawn, and disappeared from view through our front door.

·

There is nothing further, really. I lay in my room, on my bed. I had not removed my shoes. I lay on my back, unmoving, my head on the pillow, my eyes closed.

·

The door to my room also was closed, although I knew that the window remained open. I could not, of course, see the curtains as they rose softly inward, then after a few moments were sucked out and held tightly against the screen. But I could hear the wind outdoors, a sound like waves at the seashore, as it fell away, then returned to rush through the tossing, upturned leaves of the trees.

·

The house was empty around me, and, except for the noise of the wind, it was silent. I knew, however, that my grandmother would return soon from her afternoon hours of clerking at Schroeder's. She would come home, climb upstairs into her attic room, and lie down on her bed above me. I would know she was there and not know she was there.

·

My brother Julian, too, would come home from school. I would hear the quiet, faint, distant sound of his blue rubber ball as, in the back yard, he threw it up against the side of the house, then caught it, then threw it again.

·

I could see nothing, and perhaps this is why it seemed to me that I could see everything at once. In Miss Ebertson's classroom, for example, the day had ended. The room was hushed and empty. The blackboards had been washed, the window-shades drawn halfway at top and bottom against the last sunlight, the floor swept. The straight rows of desks were entirely cleared off, except that on mine, in the middle of the room, my pencils and books and notebooks lay where I had left them.

·

And yet at the same time I was still there in the room, class had not yet ended, nothing had happened to me. Ahead of me, in the row alongside the windows, Carlotta leaned her head idly on her upraised arm. Miss Ebertson continued speaking to the class—this diminutive, gray-haired, busily intense woman in tweeds who had also been my mother's teacher twenty years before. Frequently, as if time had not passed, or as if time had stopped, Miss Ebertson would confuse the two of us. She would ask for hands.

"Yes? Elizabeth?" she would say, smiling at me. Before answering, I would say quietly: "Not Elizabeth. Zoë."

.

In my room, with my eyes closed and my hands beside me on the bed, I listen to the wind.

.

For a certain time when I was in junior high school, my mother arranged for me to take lessons on the violin. During one summer I practiced each morning in the living room. Notes from my violin passed through the thin white curtains at our open windows and out into the cool, leaf-shaded air of the street.

I envied and admired Carlotta for her humor and insolence and daring, and for the way she lay upstairs on her bed reading comic books, practicing her own violin by drawing the bow, with her bare toes, back and forth across the strings.

.

Lying in my room with my eyes closed, listening to the sound of the wind in the trees outside, it seems to me that I know where everyone is. My father is a hundred miles away, driving toward home on a straight highway across the middle part of the state. The sun is shining, but off to the northwest, rising up to fill almost half of the sky, are towering storm clouds with lightning flickering low in the darkness near their bases. My father stops his car, gets out, and then stands by the open door looking toward the clouds. I can see him, alone on the long ribbon of open road, standing beside his car. He holds his hands together to form a visor over his eyes. The hot prairie wind pushes at him, billowing his shirt, fluttering the legs of his khaki trousers.

.

My grandmother lies on her bed above me. Below me, the house is empty. Outdoors, my brother bounces his ball against the high gable, its repeated sound like the distant, faint, enormously slowed beating of a heart.

.

My father is miles away on the prairie, shielding his eyes as he peers off into the northwest. In the city, somewhere on a high floor in a large building, my mother sits at a switchboard: neatly dressed, straight-backed, her eyes fixed far ahead of her at some point in the very great distance, she listens indefatigably and attentively for voices.

.

In Miss Ebertson's classroom, Carlotta sits half sideways in her seat, looking down idly at her desk: the side of her head is supported by her raised forearm, and her dark hair falls around her hand and wrist. But she also is not there; the classroom is empty and swept; and Carlotta is lying on her bed, reading, playing the violin with one bare foot, although I know that she no longer does this, that she has not played the violin for years. Then she disappears from my view, and nothing takes her place.

.

I hear the distant, faint sound of my brother's ball. The wind in the trees outside my window is like the slow sound of waves. I do not know the moment when I fall asleep. I dream once again that I am floating on the canal, in my bed, drifting slowly between embankments of high summer grass.

.

There is silence around me, a hushed, soft quietness. When I open my eyes, I see only darkness, and at first I do not know what this means, whether or not I have gone blind. Then in the faint light coming from the street lamp outdoors, I see the curtains at my window rise up gently into the room, hold there for a moment, then fall softly back.

I think to myself: It is over. Everything is all right. It is my own secret, then. I will never have to tell anything to anyone about it, ever.

III

AMBROSE, MISSOURI

I

My paternal grandfather was once mayor of Ambrose, Missouri. It was an office he held for only four years, however, failing to win it for a second term largely because of the widely held suspicion among his numerous opponents in the town that he had failed to account entirely or properly for certain public monies in his trust.

This was long ago—my grandfather was mayor from 1932 until 1936—and the case against him rose only to the level of gossip and rumor, never being either proven or disproven. I still do not know what truth there may have been in it. By the time of my own childhood and the visits I made regularly to Ambrose in the summers of the late 1940s and early 1950s, the political stage of my grandfather's life had already receded far into the past and had taken on the same comfortably exotic and distanced quality that much of the rest of Ambrose held for me as well.

A plumber by trade, my grandfather was criticized by some

—my own mother among them—for being unreliable, self-centered, and stubbornly opinionated, although I know that he treated me always, perhaps because I was his first granddaughter, with an unvaryingly indulgent kindness and charm. By the time I knew him, his working years had come to an end, and his life seemed to me as a result to be filled mainly with leisure and with a repetitive round of small daily tasks and obligations. My grandfather was a heavy drinker and smoker (he was to die, in 1960, of cancer of the throat), and in the early years of my summer visits it became a favored treat for him to take me along on his late morning or midafternoon outings to meet with his aging friends and cronies in the old taverns downtown on the main street of Ambrose—dark, varnished places that I remember as being cool, shadowy, and wonderfully cavernous, with back doors propped open toward the flowing river, places where it seems to me now that time passed with a pleasant and luxuriant slowness.

He was born into the large family of a successful farmer who had emigrated from Europe as a boy, and over the years of his own gradual social elevation in Ambrose (starting as a young man, when he set out independently in his own plumbing business), my grandfather slowly gave up workman's clothing and began to favor, even at work, wearing a tie, rumpled suit, and a brimmed hat that he tended to push well toward the back of his head, giving a suggestion at once of comfortable physical exhaustion and stylish flair. I am inclined now to imbue my grandfather with a symbolic importance, and the images I retain of him possess a simple and uncomplicated vividness. I imagine my grandfather, for example—a small man, with a homely appearance and yet a stalwart pride in his bearing—

as he steps one afternoon out of an Ambrose tavern onto the sidewalk in his rumpled suit and sweat-stained hat. And I am inclined in this image then also to see myself come out of the same door and appear beside him, incongruous and out of keeping at age six or seven or eight, two shiny barrettes in my hair, wearing a pink T-shirt, red shorts, and a pair of white summer sandals.

Ambrose was built on a steep hillside rising up from the Missouri River, and in the sultry, lingering heat of late summer afternoons, in the borrowed time just before the supper hour, my grandfather and I would make our way slowly up the hill under hanging leaves, going past the big old houses of worn brick that my grandfather told me had been, a hundred years earlier, the houses of millionaires who had been merchants, bankers, and steamboat owners. Halfway up the long hill, when my energy invariably flagged, my grandfather would put a hand in the small of my back, pushing me firmly upward, and we would continue toward home in that way, smoke trailing behind us from the cigar my grandfather held clamped in his teeth, his stained hat tilted back on his head, his free hand resting casually in the pocket of his rumpled trousers.

2

I was not born, or even yet conceived, when my newlywed mother—a bride of three months—and my grandfather met one another for the first time, at my grandparents' house in Ambrose, in March of 1940. But there is a story about the meeting that has always remained with me.

My mother, at bedtime during the first night of that long-ago visit from Three Islands with my father, caused an unsettling surprise by explaining suddenly that she preferred, in spite of the expense, to sleep not at my grandparents' house but in a room in one of the two hotels downtown. The story goes that my grandfather and she stood on either side of the already-unfolded guest bed in the living room, their voices rising sharply as they battled over a fresh sheet, my eighteen-year-old mother snatching it off the bed each time my grandfather managed to tuck it in on one side, my grandfather then reaching for it and pulling it back forcibly from my mother, until she turned and without another word to anyone went out the front door of the house and started down the hill.

I imagine this incident now in a strangely compressed and isolated way, as if it were extremely far away and I were seeing it only at the distant end of a long tunnel: my mother and my grandfather, in a small lighted area surrounded otherwise entirely by darkness, grappling fiercely in a tug of war, one of them trying to lay a white sheet on a bed, the other trying to tear it away.

3

Ambrose, because of its location on the river, was a much older town than Three Islands, having come into existence as early as the middle of the eighteenth century. It flourished most grandly in the years before the Civil War, when steamboat traffic was at its peak; then, with the coming of the railroads, the pace of the town's growth abated, and it began the long, slow continuation of its life that was to lead finally to the years of my own childhood and adolescence, when Ambrose would seem to me (or I would remember it so in adulthood) an untroubled and comfortably eventless place suspended in unbroken quietness, stillness, and deep-rooted tranquillity.

The squalor and drabness of the old town, its worn and rundown appearance, the faintly shabby look of time having passed it by—to me these were simply other aspects of what was already charmed and familiar about Ambrose, the whole of it held and captured for me indiscriminately in the humid and green-leaved stillness and heat of the deep summer seasons when I was there: the wide brown river itself, flowing toward the bottomlands and its juncture with the Mississippi and sometimes, when the water was low, sending its decaying, mud-bank smell into the lower parts of the town; the narrow main street with its uneven paving bricks; the ancient downtown buildings, some wooden and some of red brick: a grocery store, a hardware store, a tobacco store, a clothing store, a handful of taverns and the two hotels with wooden benches on the sidewalk in front of them; the tree-shaded streets making their way up the steep hill away from the river; the once-splendid millionaires' houses behind their tiny strips of lawn, their high roofs flattened at the tops and fixed with iron-filigreed widow's walks offering views of the wide and curving river below.

Farther from downtown, but still placed close together as if huddled for shelter into the side of the hill, were the plainer houses—like my grandparents' house itself, built shortly past the turn of the century, two stories high, chunky and unornamented, of plain white clapboard: its shallow porch on the front seeming all but to overhang the street; its familiar strip of thin, mossy front lawn, not more than a foot and a half or two feet deep; its old sidewalk, leading farther up the hill, buckled and cracked from the thick roots of trees growing underneath the pitted slabs of concrete.

The upstairs room I slept in when I stayed in Ambrose, on the downhill front corner of the house, was the room that had been my father and my uncle Elgar's in their boyhood, although I do not remember there being in it any discernible traces of its former inhabitants. Kept clean by my grandmother, and having been unlived in for some time, it had about it the faintly museumlike quality of almost all cared-for but seldom used spare rooms: plain and unadorned, wooden-floored, bare papered walls holding ornaments of no kind whatsoever, a small chairless table against one wall, an extra quilt folded neatly at the foot of the bed.

Into this room at night, a nearby street light shone through the hanging leaves of a great spreading tree and cast patterns of shadow and light against the walls. The front window, opened up wide to the unmoving air, was so close to the narrow street in the crowded old town that, lying awake in bed, I could hear from time to time the murmured conversations of people passing by on the sidewalk, making their way back up the hill from the taverns down by the river late at night. Sometimes I was awake even later and would hear footsteps on the hollow boards of the front porch; the careful opening of the house door; and then, after the passing of a certain time, my grandfather making his way slowly up the stairs to bed.

4

I was to learn later that in Ambrose time still existed, but that in Three Islands this was not so.

5

My grandfather was born in 1889, in a farmhouse fourteen miles outside of Ambrose, near a tiny crossroads village by the name of Brown Oak. The farm was downriver from Ambrose, on old agricultural bottomland that often became flooded in early spring, that was known for its intense and windless heat throughout the long growing months, and that endured gray winters of an ironlike cold.

A large number of stories and anecdotes at one time survived from the years of my grandfather's growing up, but few of these ever took written form, remaining instead in the memories of numerous siblings and other more distant relatives and thus dying away slowly as these people, over time, dispersed to other parts of the country, grew very old, and themselves fell gradually into silence.

I know that my grandfather was born the ninth of thirteen children who survived into adulthood, numbers suggesting that for many years near the end of the last century and for some time into the present one, the farmhouse he was born in had been filled with a great deal of life. From what I know of the family, and particularly from what I know of my great-grandfather, it is clear that the family's life was in general disciplined, orderly, and observant of the more visible proprieties of the community. At the same time, however, there was a raw and unpolished quality to life in Brown Oak, which had about it still the lingering and unkempt roughness of the back country and frontier. Some of the brothers in my grandfather's family drank in great excess, and not always well, and there were stories of quarrels, thefts, fistfights, and runaway horses. My uncle Elgar—who, unlike my father, was never to move away from Ambrose to take up a permanent life elsewhere—is fond of a surviving detail about my grandfather and his brothers: that after getting out of bed at dawn on cold winter mornings they would urinate from the upstairs windows of the farmhouse instead of going to the privy outdoors. This is a detail that my uncle Elgar continues to find amusingly hearty, although it brings to my mind instead thoughts of bare rooms, unmade bedding, and an unpleasantly damp indoor atmosphere of a gray, iron, bone-seeking cold.

For the most part I am left only with disparate images of my grandfather's childhood, some of these undoubtedly imaginary, some made up of things I have heard, and some born from impressions I collected during childhood visits to Brown Oak with my grandfather himself. I imagine him, for example—in 1895? in 1901?—walking with a number of his brothers and sisters to the schoolhouse in Brown Oak, five or six of them making their way single file under a low gray sky along the side of a road that has been made treacherous by deep wheel ruts and jagged peaks of mud frozen into a stonelike hardness. In the height of summer I see a threshing machine somewhere in the middle distance near a red barn. An iron-wheeled steam engine, black smoke belching from its chimney, drives the big thresher by means of a long, sagging belt. A cloud of chaff drifts downwind against a blue sky from the slowly growing straw stack under the gooseneck spout of the machine. Along the road, drawn slowly toward the barn by teams of large, plodding horses, come flatbed wagons piled high with bundles of grain.

6

Only much later did I come to understand precisely what it was that I felt during my repeated childhood visits to Ambrose.

My father's old bedroom, for example: empty, bare, sparsely furnished, this unused and vacant room might have been expected to awaken in me associative and derelict feelings of loneliness, abandonment, isolation, and forlornness. This was not the case, clearly; and what I understand now is that at the time of my childhood visits the wooden-floored and Spartan room was to me not an empty place but merely a natural and unquestioned part of the house, by extension a part of Ambrose itself, by even further extension a part of the countryside surrounding. The room's two open windows allowed me the soft night air, the murmur of passing voices on the sidewalk below, shadow and light from the street lamp on the corner; in the mornings came birdsong, fresh air with a sweetened coolness, sunlight through leaves, the pungent trail of my grandfather's early cigar on the shaded front porch below, the distant sound of a spoon beating against a crockery dish in the kitchen; in the

afternoon, if I lay down for a time, there was the faint movement of the thin gauze curtains, the lazily falling cry of cicadas, the ineffable and perfect stillness of a blue-hazed summer
afternoon that embraced the house and sidewalk and street, extended over the town itself, and reached outward for hundreds
and hundreds of miles in a hushed, still, poised, enchanted,
suspended, unending hour.

What I felt in Ambrose, in other words, was this: the presence of time itself, moving, continuously flowing, unending. In
Ambrose, I lived within its soft contours and in the midst of its
steady and reassuring presence, which was everywhere around
me, as sustaining and ambient as the air I breathed, the air that
faintly touched the thin white curtains of my room, and that
brought the passing murmur of voices in through my window
at night.

7

My great-grandmother died in December of 1943, in the
farmhouse in Brown Oak, having reached the age of eighty-six
and having been a widow, by that time, for thirteen years. I
know little about her except that she was born a farm daughter
from near Brown Oak, that she was seventeen years old when,
in 1874, she accepted my great-grandfather's offer of marriage,
and that she continued to live in the farmhouse until her death.

I was taken once to see her, in the early summer of 1943,
when I myself had passed my second birthday only a few
months before. Memory, of course, is untrustworthy, especially
when it has been touched by desire or imagination. It seems

impossible that I should remember that meeting with my great-grandmother, and yet from somewhere—this seems to me indelible and quite real—I have always kept a distant image of a cool, leaf-shaded porch; of people sitting in chairs around me; a small table of white wicker; and the resting arms of an ancient, seated, white-haired woman wearing a dress with rows of small pearl buttons.

After my great-grandmother's death, the farm passed out of the family's possession, and when I saw it again—I remember being driven past it by my grandfather when I was, I suppose, thirteen or fourteen years old—it looked unlike a place at all related to the past that I remembered or later came to imagine.

I don't remember my grandfather as having been in any particular way a raconteur of the past, although other members of the family—my uncle Elgar and his wife Alice, for example—seem now to think of him that way, although I suspect that they may be attributing to him a characteristic less entirely his own than one created out of their own invention and desire. I do know, however, that my grandfather took me past the old farm—probably in the summer of 1954 or 1955. And I know that I was struck then by the stark plainness of the house and by the flatness of the land that reached out in every direction around it, leaving it exposed and unprotected. The farm, when I saw it at that time, gave the impression not of being uninhabited, but very nearly so: run down and shabby, an outbuilding with weathered boards and a swaybacked roof, a rusted tractor standing in high weeds, a car pulled at an angle up to the back door of the lath-and-tarpapered house.

·

(I do not think of my grandfather now as having been a chronicler of the past. I think of him instead as having been an embodiment of it.

For many years later in his life, partly because there was almost no back yard at all in the small space behind the house in Ambrose, he kept a private vegetable garden on a tilled plot alongside the tavern and general store in Brown Oak itself. During my summertime visits, I often went along when he drove out to Brown Oak in the afternoon to pick tomatoes or corn or green beans, and my memory of him there now—standing in his garden, wearing a wide tie and his familiar rumpled suit, his worn and sweat-stained hat pushed to the back of his head—seems to me to draw together the ancient threads of history that reach far into the past and that radiate outward from his unkempt figure to the distant corners of the world.

What my troubled and unforgiving mother was least able to bear about my grandfather were the ease and unthinking confidence with which he lived comfortably and presumptively inside an unbroken flow of time, and I understand now that it was precisely this quality also that I perceived around him and in his presence when I went with him in my childhood on his afternoon trips to Brown Oak: it was this that I saw in the strangely anomalous fact of his vegetable garden's existence itself, kept carefully weeded for him by a faithful crony in Brown Oak as a result, I now suppose, of some decades-old but unforgotten political favor; in the outlandish fact, even in the middle of the garden, of my grandfather's wearing his tie and suit and his stained, ever-present hat; in the tattered screen door of the half-darkened old tavern we invariably and ritualistically went into after picking vegetables; in the familiar,

aging black dog that slept on the low wooden stoop outside
the entrance, his tail stirring idly when my grandfather paused
to scratch his ears; in the simple, echoless slap of the tavern's
closing screen door; in the all-surrounding, hushed, oppres-
sive, unending stillness of the river-bottom summer afternoons
themselves, precisely like those through which my grandfather,
time out of mind, had lived out his own long-ago childhood
summers, and no different either from that day near the end
of August in 1905, shortly after he had turned sixteen, when
my grandfather left home and walked the fourteen miles from
Brown Oak to the town of Ambrose, where he was to become apprentice to a well-digger and plumber named Caspar
Woertz, and where, gradually but surely, he was to begin his
long, determined, steady, and gratifying rise upward in life.)

8

Here is what I know of my great-grandfather, whose death-
year of 1930 has about it for me the suggestion of great antiquity.

He was born in 1845, in a small farm village not terribly
distant from Lübeck, a city at that time under the royal gover-
norship of the kingdom of Prussia. I suspect that his family was
a large one. At the age of only fourteen, with his father's permission, my great-grandfather set out for America in search,
one assumes, of the greater economic opportunities he could
expect to find there.

Some of these facts—the day, place, and year of his birth,
his age at the time of departure, the legal matter of his father's

having given permission for him to leave—are recorded in a very old document that is still in my uncle Elgar's possession in Ambrose and that the family rather loosely refers to as my great-grandfather's "passport."

This document is handwritten on thick, parchmentlike paper, in a somewhat ornate but firm German script, and is folded into quarters. It stipulates, in addition to providing the other information I have mentioned, that by leaving for America my great-grandfather will relinquish in perpetuity all of his rights and privileges as a Prussian subject, and it concludes with the date, two official signatures (but not my great-grandfather's or his own father's), and the boldly inked imprint of the circular royal stamp.

My great-grandfather carried this paper with him on his journey to America, and it is blemished noticeably by a stain of some kind which, when the paper is unfolded, covers slightly more than half of each of its quadrants, beginning at the outside corners and moving inward. Members of my family have explained the presence of the stain in different ways. My grandfather is said to have attributed its existence to sweat, although I myself never heard him speak of the paper or saw him look at it. My uncle Elgar, who displays the passport from time to time—when guests, for example, show an interest in seeing it—is fond of declaring the stain to be the result of spilled wine or beer, taking pleasure in imaginary claims of my great-grandfather's robust and precocious worldliness. As for myself, in seeking an explanation for the stain, I find that I lean unequivocally toward rainstorms and the sea.

For many years, I have preserved in secret a small number of unchanging images of my great-grandfather as a young boy of fourteen. In one of these images, for example, which as usual comes to me in silence, I know that he has just received his passport. He wears a belted jacket, and I am certain that his new passport is folded in an inside pocket of that jacket as he walks from a provincial town near Lübeck back to the small village where his family lives.

The road he follows takes him through open and gently rolling countryside. Fields of ripening barley and bearded wheat reach away from him toward distant stands of trees. At one point the road leads him directly through such a stand of trees, which I think must be birches or poplars. When this happens, he disappears from my sight for a certain time, until the road brings him out again on the other side.

On a later stretch of the road, a passing summer rainstorm darkens the sky. The sun disappears, and for some time my great-grandfather, not pausing to look for shelter, walks through a heavy rain that slants uniformly across the landscape. At last the rain stops and the sun gradually re-emerges. My great-grandfather is still walking, and heat from the sun warms his sodden clothing. He removes his belted jacket and carries it flung over his shoulder. Here and there, small curls of mist rise up from the drying road.

.

(When he left Europe, my great-grandfather did so from a North Sea port, in late summer. Of the very moment of his departure itself, I imagine these things: a sudden flurry, a discernible increase in noise and activity on the crowded pier; commands being shouted back and forth in a language that I can hear but cannot understand; the freeing of hawsers; gulls screaming as they rise up into the air; and a widening strip of black water seen far below by my great-grandfather, standing at the rail, as the vast side of the ship draws slowly away.

.

That the crossing was storm-tossed, of course, is also entirely possible. It may very well be, in mid-Atlantic, that smooth, deep, green swells arose, and then that a screaming wind tore away their crests, filling the air with whiteness and spume. There could have been shuddering blows against the bow of the laboring ship, its gutters and decks flowing knee-deep in seawater that found its way down even into the dampened quarters far below, where my great-grandfather, lying in his tiny, narrow bunk, wearing the same belted jacket as before, listened to the muted howl of the wind, and felt beneath him the deep, churning, heaving flanks of the sea.

.

I know that my great-grandfather did not arrive in the port of New York, but that he came around instead by way of New Orleans, where he penetrated America from the bottom of the continent. I am quite certain that at some point during this stage of his journey, again, there was rain.

As he came upriver by steamboat, the weather remained summerlike and warm. During the balmy daytime hours, my great-grandfather stood for long periods at the crowded rail of the boat, watching the wide river pass slowly by and the forested land on the far shore recede gradually southward. At night, he slept on the deck. My great-grandfather would search for an untaken space or corner, perhaps somewhere next to a cabin wall, and he would use his thick cloth traveling bag for a pillow.

I believe it to have been somewhere between Memphis and

Sainte Genevieve, in the hours after midnight and before dawn, that a thunderstorm arose, illuminating the broad expanse of the suddenly windswept river, then sending peals of thunder and sheets of rain against the boat, obscuring from view, except dimly and briefly in the wild flashes of lightning, its slowly turning stern wheel, and the smoke being snatched away from its high, twin stacks.

.

My great-grandfather reached St. Louis in late September of 1859, by which time, in exchange for money or food, he had bartered away both his cloth traveling bag and its contents, with the exception of a small number of personal possessions that he carried either in his pockets or in a knotted handkerchief.

How he traveled the forty miles from St. Louis to Ambrose, I don't know; nor do I know with certainty how he made his way later from Ambrose to the black-dirt region of Brown Oak, near the point in the bottomland where the Missouri River joins the Mississippi.

I do know, however, that from the time of his arrival in Brown Oak, my great-grandfather succeeded in finding work as a hired farmhand; that he continued to work as a hired hand through his teens and into his early adulthood; that he gained a reputation for being hardworking and reliable, and even more for being a conscientious saver of the money he earned.

I know that in his middle twenties, after a decade of working for hire, he was able to buy his own section of land and begin to farm it; that he built a barn on this property and then, in the years following, a house; that in 1874, when he was twenty-nine years old, he married, taking as his bride a girl who was twelve years younger than himself; and that my great-grandparents' marriage, over the next twenty-three years, was to produce a family of thirteen children who would survive into adulthood, as well as an additional, smaller, number who would not.

.

(I know this, in other words: that years gradually accumulated; that decades went by; that the century turned; that a new set of numbers began their incremental and implacable count.

And then something happened. When my great-grandfather's long, backward-reaching life came to an end in 1930—a date, as I have said, that itself seems to me now touched by great antiquity—something began that I think of as a waiting period, a time suspended in quietness, a long, held breath. This attenuated moment, this span of somehow motionless time between the movement of two eras, the particular, scarcely breathing quality of those years from 1930 to 1943, may in fact have existed only in symbol, or perhaps the greater truth is that it existed nowhere other than in the particular history of my own family. And yet I am absolutely certain, however that may be, that the moment when it came to an end was sometime near that day in the early summer of 1943, when, reaching backward through time itself, I touched my great-grandmother and, through her, touched my departed great-grandfather, in that way establishing a continuity from his life to my own: the day when, I know, these being preserved from somewhere in the earliest and most distant reaches of my consciousness, I remember a cool, leaf-shaded porch; people sitting on chairs and talking quietly; a table of white wicker; and the extended arms of my ancient, seated, white-haired great-grandmother, who wore, only a few months before her death, a long white dress with concise, parallel rows of small pearl buttons.))

Notes.

1. There was, in other words, a hole in time. Some were successful in not falling into it. Among these, on my father's side, were my great-grandmother herself, my grandfather and my grandmother, my uncle Elgar, and, in her way, his sister Denitia. My mother, however, from the other side of my family, was one of those unable to reach the other side, but one who fell down instead into the measureless abyss of emptiness without time. When my father met her at the boardinghouse door in Three Islands, in the middle of a silent afternoon in July of 1939, she was there already, and it was then that she drew him in after her.

2. My mother, clearly, could not exist in Ambrose, for the obvious reason that the people around her there continued to move within the sustaining current of time. This helps to explain more exactly:

a) the symbolism underlying my mother's first and prototypic struggle with my grandfather: when he attempted to place the sheet on the bed and she, just as willfully and unrelentingly, tore it repeatedly away;

b) and this: that on the cool, leaf-shaded porch, I know for a given fact that my mother was one of those sitting in chairs around me. That in my memory, however, search as I might, she is not there; I am unable to find her; she is wholly absent.

3. As for my father, of course, when he lived in Ambrose, he lived still within time. Only later, a short period after his arrival in Three Islands, did he enter the world of its absence. This makes it possible for me to understand why his old room in Ambrose, where I slept, was empty and yet not empty.

.

(My grandfather's death from cancer of the throat occurred on the eleventh of May in 1960, when I was completing my first year of college in West Tree, Minnesota. The first news of the certainty of his approaching death, however, and of the precise and deadly nature of his rapidly progressing illness, reached our house in Three Islands somewhat less than a year earlier, on August 28th, 1959, when my father returned from a brief visit by himself to Ambrose. On the evening of his homecoming, and in fact only some few moments after it, before my father had changed out of his traveling clothes, I saw, through an open door in the upstairs of our house, my parents engaged in sexual intercourse on the edge of their bed. This moment, I think now, exists as the turning point of my understanding. And yet that the door was standing open; the significance of its having been left so; and the even greater significance of my chance passing by and looking through it to see my parents engaged, at just that time, in that act—these were things that would become explicable to me only some time later; only after the difficult attaining of my understanding of the hole in time; only after I at last understood how it was that my mother could be swept into ecstasy, as I saw that night, by the terrible and soothing and quietly whispered promises of death.

.

(After my father graduated from high school, in 1935, he continued for some time to remain associated with my grandfather in Ambrose as a plumber, although this work at the time was unreliable and intermittent. He gave thought to leaving home, but he found a position instead as day laborer in the completion of a new steel bridge five miles upriver from Ambrose. He paid a fellow worker, after hours, to teach him to be a welder. For another eighteen months he found a place as construction worker on a lock and dam system not far downriver past Brown Oak, driving every day the twenty miles each way from Ambrose and return.

In the early spring of 1939, my father found himself out of work, and he struck an agreement with my grandfather to enlarge the rough earthen cellar under the house in Ambrose and to finish it with a concrete floor and walls. When the job was finished six weeks later, however, my grandfather, having recently lost a large amount of money at cards, declared himself unable to pay, although, as usual, without explicitly declaring the reason.

I have often imagined my father and my grandfather, one morning in early June of 1939, standing on the sidewalk in front of the house. I think of this—the moment when I see them—as being the precise moment when my father made his decision once and for all to leave Ambrose. My grandfather stands with his feet slightly apart, his hands resting deeply in the pockets of his old suit jacket, his brimmed hat pushed back on his head. My young father, an inch or so the taller, stands beside and somewhat in front of him, looking at him, waiting for an answer that does not come. Then he turns and walks away.

I imagine that my grandfather remains there for some time, alone on the sidewalk, his hands in his pockets, looking up at the house.

As for my father: he drives north on the long, straight, flat highway to Three Islands; he takes a room over Jarchow's grocery at Third Street and Central Avenue; he meets my uncle Victor one night in the tavern; and he sits alone on the front steps of the boardinghouse by the canal until at last, from the far end of the block, my grandmother appears and makes her way slowly toward him, a shopping bag hanging down from each of her hands, wearing a dark print dress and a hat with a large, pearl-tipped pin.))

IV

WEST TREE, MINNESOTA

PROLOGUE

By great good fortune, I arrived at the College of West Tree in the last few years that remained before its character was to change forever.

When I arrived at West Tree in the autumn of 1959, a century of its history had passed. These hundred years had of course first seen the conception of the college and its early growth, but then, equally and perhaps even more important, they had endowed it with a generous plenitude of slowly passing decades during which nothing was required of it other than that it remain as it was and allow itself to be more perfectly formed by the work of time: to mellow and age, to become gradually softened and worn, to steep in the sun-warmed redolence of its endlessly repetitive, quietly reflective, essentially unchanging existence.

I had the good fortune, in other words, to be a student there in the small handful of years that marked the institution's brief moment of greatest and most profound maturity.

.

I am struck that those who speak most earnestly about the high importance of education are among that number most eager also to assert of education that it is "a living thing." Whether itself valid or not, the premise leads to a corollary voiced most commonly in phrases such as "the living past," "our living heritage," and "living bodies of knowledge." I depart from these analysts and register my contention that the corollary is imperceptive and fallacious, as its being dressed in the threadbare robes of cliché may suggest.

Certainly it is far more evident that what truly vitalizes education toward the baccalaureate is precisely the fact that, as it occurs, one dwells in the company not of the living, but of the dead. Consider for a moment a young person's experience in first entering into the membership of an ancient college, and scrutinize the exact nature of that new student's surroundings. The stature, quietness, poise, and resonance; the dignity and prestige; the stability, calmness, reverence, ceremony, and tradition; the rare and treasured whispers of profundity; even the texture and the very scent and feel themselves of gaining an education—it seems to me that every one of these things exists precisely because, as a student, one lives within the very rooms and halls, passes through the very doors, makes one's way along the paths, not of the living but of the dead: of those who have gone before; those who are no longer here; those who may or may not have left something behind.

—Professor Gilbert Charles
Durham, DLitt, *A Philosophic
Etiology of the Baccalaureate*
(Baltimore, 1927), pp. 17–18

·

Notes.

1. The first member of my family to go to college, I left at home behind me fear, uncertainty, and approaching death. I did not yet know what field of study I would take up.

2. My initial sight of the town of West Tree, on September 2nd, 1959, came to me from a window of the train I rode on as it turned to follow a curve in the small prairie river approaching from the south. From a mile or so away, as it came into view, the town revealed itself to me where it lay on the twin low banks of the river in afternoon sunlight. A scattering of church steeples penetrated through a canopy of thick foliage that, in those very earliest days of autumn, clung to its heavy summertime density of a deep, luxuriant green.

3. The college itself stood a short distance beyond the northeast edge of West Tree, separated from the town also by merit of its standing at least in part on a softly rounded prairie hill that gave it a slight but noticeable rise in elevation. The brick structures and stone pilings of the college's buildings, obscured by trees and late-summer foliage, revealed themselves to me in glimpses as I made my way toward them from the train station near the center of the town, my imagination being supplied

only gradually with an emerging sense of the whole. I saw a turret here and there, and some distance away a high tower of gray stone. Through the leaves, there appeared nearby a slope or two of tiled roof. For a time, I had an unobstructed view of the upper floor and roof of what I took to be a very old building, square in shape, of softened red brick, surmounted by a wooden tower on each of whose sides was a clock face with shapely black hands. I imagined these tower clocks—themselves unsheltered, exposed without respite to the light and heat of the sun—as gazing down like mentors and guards over shaded walkways and across quiet, spreading lawns in the old, time-worn interior of the campus itself.

4. The day of my arrival was poised, warm, summerlike, and calm. As I made my way up the hill, carrying my suitcase first in one hand and then the other, there was silence all around me. Briefly, at the top of the hill, I walked on level ground in unbroken sunlight. Then I entered in under the shade of trees.

I

I

The building I lived in stood among spreading shade trees on a wide expanse of flat ground from which it seemed to rise up naturally as an imposing and yet modest structure. Three stories high, of a comfortably weathered gray brick, it allowed the eye to move casually upward toward a gabled roof forested by symmetrical groupings of high and ornate yet sentinel-like chimneys. I came to cherish this building, finding an unpretentious and sustaining dignity in its proportioned expression of extreme simplicity and quietly unassuming elegance.

·

Perhaps for these reasons, the building seemed to me to exist in an alluringly secure and inviolable harmony with its surroundings. There was invariably, I came to feel, an elemental stillness, a feeling of immutably harbored safety, inside it—even at those times, for example, when thunder fell down in mountainous, unceasing avalanches from the nighttime sky, when rain lashed against the darkened window of my single room, and when a flailing wind, lightning-brightened, screamed its way through the clusters of chimneys on the rain-swept roof.

The old building appeared to me permanent and unchanging, yet filled with a remarkable subtlety and variety of expressiveness. With a compliantly yielding, venerable equanimity, it waited patiently as snow piled up deeply on its stairways, window ledges, and step-railings; or it endured stoically the brick-darkening streaks of day-long rains driven on the cold winds of March or early April; or, with its various entrance-way doors set open wide, it seemed itself actually to become a part of the quiet, sweet, harvest-scented warmth of certain poised and circumambient autumn afternoons, when for a few perfect hours the air that came in at its windows and drifted through its long, high corridors would seem as enchanted and timeless, I imagined, as feeling or thought or eternity itself.

.

My own room was small, on the second floor, its window facing westward and providing me with a view, across smooth lawns and tree-shaded walkways, of the interior and most perfectly sheltered part of the campus. Like all the rooms in the old building, mine contained vestiges of a distant past that could be put to such use as an occupant might choose. The small fireplace in the wall across from my bed had been bricked in carefully and painted over. Its mantelpiece, however, served conveniently as a bookshelf, and on the narrow, green-tiled hearth set into the wooden floor below, as if they were warming their toes at the memory of a fire there, I placed my boots and slippers and shoes in a row. Flanking the fireplace, not quite halfway up toward the high ceiling, two unused gas jets extended from the wall. One of these became a coat hook, the other a place for my night clothes and robe. The room, like the rest of the building's interior, smelled pleasantly of old wood, fresh paint, and new wax, an assembly of odors—memorable to me even now—redolent at once of the freshly scrubbed and of the distant, unreachable, beckoningly ancient.

.

(If, in the late evening hours, I were to open the door of my room and peer out into the wide interior corridor, I would see the hall monitor (a student like myself) at the far end, seated at a small wooden table that held a shaded lamp, her face bent over the pages of a book, and her hair, as likely as not, falling over the upraised forearm against which she rested her head.

If much later, in the very deepest hours of the night, I were to open the door and peer out once again, I would find, in the half-lit hallway, an unqualified perfection and purity of absence and silence: the nearby curve of the white-painted bannister descending from the shadowy floor above mine, and, in turn, to the shadowy floor below; the narrow runner of thin carpet leading away from me, smoothly waxed wood gleaming on either side of it; and, far down at the distant end, the empty table at which the monitor had sat, its surface now bare, the shaded lamp burning steadily in the hushed, untenanted, half-gathered gloom.)

Notes.

1. Only very gradually and through a series of fortuitous accidents would it be revealed to me, and then at first only dimly, that my studies at West Tree were to concern themselves in the end with the nature of time and space.

2. Of immeasurable importance to me in my coming later to understand and embark upon my true choice of study was the window of my room. This window offered, of course, a number of pleasures and conveniences, but of greatest significance was the fact that its westward exposure took advantage of the prevailing westerly breezes, with the result that, at any time of day or night, if I were to raise the window even slightly, a gentle flow of air would come steadily into my room, enabling me to sit or kneel at this opening for as long as I wished and breathe deeply into my lungs the life-giving sweetness of the moving air, and through it—as I would come to know and understand only later—antiquity itself, the history of history.

3. That I at first felt homesick there was no question, and often in this early period, at day's end, at my window, gazing toward stone buildings half obscured in gathering and sweet-scented darkness, I thought of my family. Hundreds of miles away, beyond the reach of hearing or touch or sight, I imagined them as they might be at that precise, exact moment. My grandmother, on her bed, gazing toward the ceiling of her attic room; my mother cutting vegetables, in despair, in the kitchen; my father reading his newspaper in the living room; my brother, in the back yard, bouncing his ball in the last fading light high against the pointed gable of the house, catching it as it came down, then throwing it up yet again. (In Ambrose, as far away again to the south, removed from me still more distantly by the falling curve of the earth, my grandfather sat down on the edge of his bed, then allowed himself slowly to lie back against his pillows.)

II

I began, then, at this time in my life, to study in earnest; therefore I gradually fell also, at the same time, into the language and words of study.

2

I

Of course a number of alterations had been made in the college since its beginning. In general, however, such changes were minor—the elimination of hitching posts, for example, or the paving of streets—and even some of those that were larger in scope had been brought into existence long enough ago that they also had taken on the college's worn atmosphere of reflective timelessness, even if it was impossible for them (unlike the ancient building where I had my room) to claim their origins in the years of most remote and therefore most pure antiquity.

.

Such was the case, for example, of the building devoted to the study of the physical and natural sciences, a hall constructed in 1921, at a time when something more than half of the college's present life had already passed by. But by the time of my own arrival at West Tree, the science hall had aged just enough to allow it to blend almost without disjuncture into the venerable physical document that made up the college as a whole, and thus also into the overall experience of the past that I found myself deliberately seeking out, an experience that I believed myself not only invited but intended to gain as the central part of my life as a student there.

I was not to become a student of the sciences except in the most limited way, and yet the old hall revealed to me some idea of the appeal and remarkable complexity the sciences might offer to those inclined to take up their study. The building's wide central corridor was lined generously with display cases suggesting the range, variety, and agedness of this heritage. Small stuffed mammals with tiny black eyes and sharp claws, birds perched in their colorful plumage, displays of multi-colored mineral samples and rows of glittering crystals held my attention for more than one long afternoon during my early time at the college when, endeavoring to expose myself to the campus's varied offerings, I lingered with my notebook before these display cases with the idea of opening myself up at least to some conception, and recording it if possible, of the enduring significance they might hold for me.

In the second, upstairs, corridor of the building were displayed in glass jars a variety of creatures (and parts of creatures) that had once been living but now without exception were hairless, pale, and suspended in transparent liquid. Among these was a collection of embryos, including a human embryo of three and a half inches or so in length, its scarcely formed arms held open before its top-heavy and bowed head as if in anticipation of embracing some presence that had not appeared to it and that seemed to me, under the circumstances, unlikely now ever to do so.

The interest these display cases held for me—even more so here, on the less frequently visited second floor of the building—was heightened by their appearance of having not been touched or altered for a great many years. In their striking desuetude they seemed to me in a number of subtle ways more evocative than might have been the case had they been attended to diligently, and for a number of long hours, holding my notebook, I studied them closely. In a display case at the farthest end of the hallway, I remember, there hung a lanky and brownish skeleton that, after long solitude, had lost both of its arms, those limbs having fallen away to lie crumpled and hapless near the skeleton's dangling and bony feet. And my attention was captured, in a poorly lighted area at the other end of the hall, by a display of five brains of graduated sizes in an equal number of smooth-domed glass jars wearing caps of thin gray dust and standing in a descending row on their varnished wooden bases, leading me to wonder how long ago, and by what solicitously attending hand, itself perhaps antiquated by now also into dust, they might have once been placed so carefully there.

II

Near this time, perhaps in part as a result of other events that were taking place in my life, and perhaps as a result also of the increasingly demanding introspection and close analysis that were being required of me now at West Tree, the idea first revealed itself to me, faintly, that my studies were destined to take the form of the discovery of things through their absence.

As this perception took hold and grew, I made an effort to explore it further by allowing myself exposure to other areas of the curriculum that, like science, might in the end prove of lesser interest to me but whose merit, complexity, and significance I could easily perceive for those who elected to follow them. In my exploration of the gymnasium, for example, I entered a world of the mind that showed me at first only a number of the same things I had seen in the science building: yet here I was to be guided even more helpfully on the path toward my own chosen studies.

·

Built in 1905 (thirty-five years later than my own building), the gymnasium was a broad structure of warm, age-softened red brick, although its interior revealed in various places a supporting structure of riveted iron beams, numerous of these having been painted white so many times over the years that they had achieved the smoothness and color of thick cream, while this ponderous frame rested (these could be seen in the basement levels) on bulging, uneven, fortress-thick foundations and interior supporting walls of boulders, ancient mortar, and crushed stone.

The airy and wooden-floored basketball court itself (surrounded by high, cathedral-like windows covered by wire grilles) was of less immediate interest to me than were some of the more secluded parts of the building. On the topmost floor, for example, I came upon a wood-paneled corridor that gave the impression of no longer ever being visited, as if the function it once served (as a passage, perhaps, to the offices of the faculty of athletics) had since been diverted entirely elsewhere.

Here, I once again found long rows of display cases, fitted two-thirds of the way up to the ceiling against the length of one wall; and, in a number of lingering and undetected visits to these far upper reaches of the old building, I took it upon myself to study their contents as attentively as I was able.

Without question, the offerings here were infinitely less rich than those in the science hall, although I was to become aware that this relative simplicity was not to keep them from revealing an even greater significance.

It was obvious to me from the beginning, however, that the objects here, in and of themselves, could realistically be of no conceivable interest to anyone. Minerals, embryos, varied species of mammals and reptiles and birds—these possessed a significance needing no explanation; but before me here were only abandoned and desiccated husks alluding to no principle of ongoing organic creation, and suggesting no hint, however faint, of any natural complexity or evolution. Instead of rows of geodes and crystals, here were rows of old leather footballs that, having long since lost their air, had collapsed absurdly in on themselves, becoming pathetic bits of discolored, cracked, largely oxidized detritus. Instead of embryos or inner organs or human brains preserved in transparent fluid, here, placed foolishly on small wooden pedestals, were antique baseballs—stained, bulging, their stitches broken, in some cases their once-compact insides escaping slowly in abundant and useless coilings.

Even so, in spite of the forlorn, derelict, and almost clownish tone of these poor display cases, there was at the same time an atmosphere in the old corridor that drew me back to it repeatedly, invariably at a warm and hushed period of the day when, owing to the direction the windows of the hallway faced, streaks of late-afternoon sunlight fell lazily over its wooden floor. In retrospect my gratitude that I returned as I did is immeasurable, for on one of those afternoons a distinction came to me—inexplicably and unexpectedly—that I think of now as marking my first moment of independent thought during my time at West Tree, and as marking the turning point also from which I was to follow, perhaps inevitably, the previously unseen path toward my own true studies. The moment of my insight was accompanied by a feeling simultaneously of excitement and faint alarm. Pushing myself up, as if through the shock of some invisible summons, from the place where I had been sitting on the floor with my back against the wall, experiencing at the same moment an oddly painful quickening of my pulse and shallowness in my breathing, I stepped quickly to one of the windows nearby, braced my notebook on its sill, and, the unsteadiness of my hand necessitating that I do so at once a second time immediately afterward, I wrote:

> Science is the study of what is.
> Athletics is the study of what has been.
>
> Science is the study of what is.
> Athletics is the study of what has been.

Notes.

1. The museumlike silence of the corridor I sat in; the paths of sunlight lying across the floor; the tiered photographs of mustachioed athletes staring out at me with the faces of dead men; the old dates written on various of the decayed and mummified objects in the cases—1891, 1902, 1921, 1928: all of these things must have contributed to my coming suddenly to under-

stand that in the gymnasium I was in fact visitor to a place where meaning was created not by the living but by the dead.

This idea having become clear to me, I understood as well, and almost instantly, what it was about the atmosphere of the gymnasium that had drawn me back to it again and again in the silence of those late afternoons: I had returned, I understood now, because here was a house of scholarship in which meaning was determined not by the presence of things, but by their absence.

2. Neither in childhood nor in adolescence had I been one who felt a natural inclination toward athletic games or participation in them, not having understood clearly the exact nature of their significance (something about which others had seemed so unthinkingly, intuitively, even rudely confident). Now, however, it seemed to me that at long last I understood this aspect of the matter with a clarity that was both inescapable and luminously revealing. The meaning of athletic games, I now understood, was created entirely through the fact of their having been played before, and by no other cause. And those who had brought this meaning into existence, who had played the games before, whose few varied and paltry remains decayed slowly in the unvisited corridor where I now sat, were themselves, demonstrably and patently and obviously, also now gone.

3. It had seemed to me earlier that the forlorn and desiccated objects in the display cases before me possessed, if anything, only the quaint eloquence of an imprisoned and eternal muteness. Now, however, I saw that the truth was in fact profoundly otherwise: that the dead were not voiceless at all.

As a young girl growing up in Three Islands, I had long ago

heard the shouts of players. In softball games on the empty lot by the canal, for example, on cicada-filled summer afternoons, I had listened to their cries. In high school, I had heard the autumn-crisp sounds of football, and, on winter nights, the muted roar that came from behind the closed doors of the school gymnasium. And now, too, at West Tree, especially at the close of certain warm days in spring or fall, when the air had fallen absolutely still, I was to hear again, at the window of my room, those same distant voices—the far-off shouts of players from the level fields below the main part of the campus: the faint cheers, the briefly audible and then falling cries, the distant, impassioned urgings—and I was to understand in a way that I had never understood before, with a radiant and lucid clarity, this fact: that coming to my ears, all along, had been nothing other than the voices of the dead themselves.

These were sounds, indisputably, that came from living throats, but what significance could they possibly hold unless they were sounds, otherwise without meaning, that had arisen first, in their very inception, from the straining lungs and shaping mouths of the dead? The games themselves would not exist if the dead had not created them; the rules by which the games were played were the rules of the dead; the distances to be run, heights to be jumped, records to be achieved and broken: these were the distances, heights, and achievements first marked and determined not by the living but by the dead. Those who now took up athletics as their field of study were themselves, then, animated by the dead; and their urgent voices, having been given birth through a medium of absence and silence, were in fact an audible chorus made manifest and given life from beyond the grave.

4. I remember vividly my first clear understanding of these sounds at West Tree, coming as it did at the end of my final visit to the upstairs hallway of the old gymnasium.

I had remained in the corridor later than usual, sitting in my place against the wall until the familiar streaks of afternoon sunlight had lifted themselves up from the floor and begun to climb the glass panes of the display cases, illuminating the artifacts and photographs there before rising even farther, reaching for a time into the high corners under the ceiling, and then, after a period of four or five held breaths, rapidly losing color and warmth and fading away entirely.

Near this same time, I heard shouts and echoing cries that seemed to come to me from a great distance, that rose up around me as if from no particular direction before falling abruptly into silence and then lifting slowly so I could hear them again faintly, then more audibly once more, although they still came as if from no clear direction.

Leaving the hallway and making my way down the darkened staircase toward the lighted areas below, I doubted at first that I was coming closer to the origin of the sounds; after descending another level, however, it seemed to me that I was approaching nearer, and by the time I had come to the deepest (and most brightly lighted although windowless) part of the massive old building, among its cellar walls of bulging stone and old mortar, it was clear to me that the voices came from beyond an arched doorway that stood open, marked overhead by a wooden sign with the word NATATORIUM stenciled in black letters. Looking into this doorway, I saw that it opened into a room filled with metal lockers and painted wooden benches, and that at that room's far end stood another, wider, archway, this time with NATATORIUM curving in bold, mosaic-tiled letters over its top. It was through this second archway (as I would soon experience for myself) that one went still farther down a frail iron staircase into the antique, cavernous swimming chamber that occupied its brightly lighted and echo-filled place in the very deepest recesses of the old gymnasium, and from which the shouting voices I had heard had risen up to me, faintly and distantly and waveringly, in the hallway far overhead.

5. I did not, at this time, go into the locker room, pass through the second archway, and stand at the top rail of the high iron stair gazing down, since those in the pool were men, swimming unclothed, and my presence, out of keeping with convention, would have been only disruptive and unwelcome. As it happened, however, the curriculum at West Tree held as an ancient and unquestioned tenet that women enrolled there should fulfill a requirement early in their first term either developing or perfecting an ability to swim with at least a moderate degree of expertise, for the purpose of demonstrating their ability, should this ever become necessary, to save themselves from drowning. As a result, very shortly after my discovery of the natatorium, I found myself once again in the subterranean levels of the gymnasium, entering the open outer door, passing through the wider archway, and, from the bottommost platform of the suspended iron stairway, actually diving into the crowded, warm, blue water of the antique pool and, as I did so (and as I broke up once again through its tossing surface), releasing the sound of my own voice out into the moist air, causing that voice, among the others, to echo and reverberate from the iron beams overhead, from the expanses of the

high vaulted ceiling, from the beige-tiled walls that pressed in around the edges of the pool, quaint and old-fashioned with their mosaic ornamentation of green leaves, curling tendrils, and blushing, pink, lotuslike flowers.

The experience, of course, as I was later to understand more fully, provided a significant step forward in the process of my education; and the awareness did not escape me, as I swam, that what I had recognized earlier as the voices of the dead would now once again, at this very moment, be rising up through ventilating shafts or through unknown and secret hollows in the thick ancient walls, into the distant corridor where I first had heard them. And I knew as well, had I somehow been sitting there once more, that I would have heard them again as before, elusive, suggestive, profound with distant meaning; but that now my own raised voice (as I broke up over and over through the tossing waters of the crowded and turbulent pool) would itself be woven, inextricably, among them.

III

A great deal happened to me during the brief but intense period of my exposure to athletics; and I know with certainty that in the time covered by my program in swimming, when I entered the pool faithfully each afternoon, I grew to understand clearly the attraction so many others found in the embrace of athletics: the comforting strength and the deep, communal, uplifting steadiness of one's relation to the dead that were to be found within the world of active, effortful, organized sport.

During this period, as I examined the possibility that I might myself choose to take up the study of athletics, I spent considerable time in solitary visits to remote corners of the campus in order to study more closely some of the varied possibilities for achievement, perception, and communion-like understanding that could be open to me as a scholar of this kind: the raising of the shouts and cries of the dead, for example, up into the high, thin rafters of the basketball court; the offering of them into a cool evening mist as darkness descended over the last stretch of cinder track down near the river; or even the heedless flinging of them up into the bright high vault of crystalline blue sky itself, over green playing fields warmed by the autumn sun and sweetened to a pleasure almost beyond endurance by the mingled scents of earth, bruised grass, and drying leaves.

·

And yet it became, in part, those very cries and voices that would contribute so soon to the erosion of my interest in athletics, although it was true that I continued always afterward to listen to them with the nostalgic pleasure of an old and once-intimate friend—when, for example, at the window of my room, I would hear their faraway sound carried to me once again on the still air of quiet afternoons in autumn or spring.

But what soon became obvious to me, even so, were the single-dimensioned narrowness, the invariable, fixed, and unchanging sameness of these trained and devoted songs of absence. They were voices, I understood absolutely, that drew their vitality and their very being from the dead. But what more than this absolute and primal truth—that the dead were utterly gone—were they capable of revealing to me further about the world of absence from which they arose?

Through athletics I had by now come to know with certainty, as I had only sensed before, that my studies were to take the form of the discovery of things through their absence: by means of athletics, after all, I had first heard the voices of the dead, had chosen to follow where they led, had given my own voice over to their chorus, had been guided swiftly to a deepened knowledge. For all these things I was grateful. And yet even so, in my continuing desire for the entire truth, was it wholly thankless of me now to imagine that those familiar and guiding sounds themselves might be allowed to dissipate into nothingness, and that, through their replacement by silence, I might be free to step forward and become more intimately acquainted, not merely with what the voices could tell me, but with the very reality of the absence that had brought them into existence?

Notes.

1. I became aware at the same time that something within my nature was inclined less toward motion than it was toward stillness. During the period of my afternoon program in swimming, I soon discovered that what moved me most deeply were not the strenuous exertions themselves of acting out ritualized movements of the dead—diving into the water, holding my breath until my lungs cried out in pain, straining my limbs to a trembling exhaustion in contests through the spume-tossed, archaic waters of the pool; but rather the stillness, quietude, and serenity that invariably followed: when, in my room once again, at the desk facing my window, dressed in dry clothing, I would feel for a certain time as if I were resting quietly at the center of all things, as if, in the calm after motion and noise, tendrils were flung out from my room in every direction to the farthest reaches of the earth, forming unseen and living

connections between me and all things everywhere, making it undesirable and unnecessary for me ever again so much as to speak, or to move, or to stir.

2. By my own nature and by the direction of my thinking, then, it became obvious to me that I could not possibly continue further with my studies in athletics. I understood clearly now that if shouts and voices were removed from athletics, as I desired them to be, the very meaning of athletics would be removed as well; and that if movement were taken away from them, they themselves would disappear entirely.

3. Often in these ruminative periods after swimming, I found that I was visited by thoughts of my family. These thoughts remained with me vividly for some time and returned often.

.

How they were organized, however, is difficult to describe accurately, since they presented themselves to me in so great a variety of guises and images, coming toward my room from such distances, and arriving in so overlapping an abundance, that they seemed to me to take place not singly, but with a simultaneity that, had there been sound to accompany them, would in its result have been deafening, thunderous, and massive.

I saw, however, that they occurred without so much as a whisper, a stirring, or a word. This meant, I began to perceive, that all of them were gone.

.

In time, because these thoughts returned to me frequently, I found myself discerning patterns within them, faint shapings, repeated but not identical glimpsings of movement that were quickly closed away from my sight, although sometimes they remained longer, like slowly fading after-images, in some half-obscured part of my memory. On certain rare occasions, movements of this kind would fall into patterns suggesting the presence of clearer relationships, and these I would seize onto more forcibly and attempt to hold, seeing and studying them later in my memory, where, unrooted from time, they existed (as I grew slowly to understand) not chronologically but in a single, recurring moment: my great-grandfather, in a belted jacket, walking on a country road in Prussia one day in 1859; my grandfather, in 1905, making his way on foot one summer afternoon from Brown Oak to Ambrose; my father, in 1939, driving on the long, straight, flat, two-lane highway from Ambrose to Three Islands; my parents, on the night when news came of my grandfather's nearing death, in their upstairs bedroom in our house in Three Islands, on the edge of the bed, my mother's fingers digging into the bedcover in the visible seizing of her blindly unheeding ecstasy; and I, Zoë Handke, on September 24th, 1959, far away to the north, in West Tree, Minnesota, during the evening dinner hour, in gathering darkness, at my desk, in silence, looking out of my window across the smooth, wide, empty, cool, swiftly darkening lawns of the college.

IV

(From the window of my room, far across the widest reach of the college's central yard, I was able to see the hall for the humanities. This was the same square building of weather-softened red brick whose wooden clock tower and angled roof

I had glimpsed through the foliage on the day of my first approach to the campus.

From my earliest awareness of it (I gazed toward it often from my desk at the window), I had found myself drawn by the sight of this building, and through good fortune I was led, at this time, to become acquainted with it more intimately.

I cannot easily overstate the importance of that experience, for not only, inside the walls of this austere old building, was I to come upon architectural characteristics more antique even than those in the deepest levels of the gymnasium; but I was to find myself entering also the inner chambers of a way of study that was to lead me at last (although I could not have known this at the time) toward the culmination of my search for a perfected way of understanding.

.

Built in 1870 (making it the same age as the building I roomed in), the hall for the humanities stood on a slight rise in the earth, unshaded by trees, in a noticeable but unpretentious degree of isolation. Unusual among the college buildings, it possessed (due in part to its placement on the small rise) an unobstructed view to the west. From its front steps, or from certain of its windows inside, one could look out over the tree-lined course of the small river below that made its way through West Tree, over the few clustered rooftops of the town itself that were visible somewhat farther away, and then on for mile beyond mile over the rolling prairie that reached outward, sealike and yet without movement, to the vanishing point of the horizon.

This quality of exposure and isolation, the remarkable austerity of the building, its weathered plainness—these commanded my attention from the beginning. With an equal strength, too, I was attracted by the sheer fact of the old hall's great antiquity, which evoked for me with forcefulness the treasurable qualities of motionlessness, absence, and silence. So simple a thing, for example, as the hollows worn into the unpolished brown stone of its front steps—making basins that now held small, tiered pools of water after passing rains—summoned up for me with a powerful awareness the foot-falls and steps of the countless others who had climbed there before me and who now were gone; just as the ponderous, old-fashioned door handle of brass, with its broad and deeply saddled thumb latch, called forth invariably the hands of those who had entered this same doorway before me, and who now long since had receded into a distant and unfleshed muteness far beyond the grave.

Inside the building as well, absence after absence greeted me. Allowing the heavy wooden door to settle into its frame behind me, I found myself surrounded inside by an unbroken silence, muteness, and quietness, and it became clear to me at once that I had entered here a different manner of place altogether, in its very essence, from the hall of science or the old gymnasium.

Here, after all, were none of the accoutrements or objects of those earlier places. Here I saw no glass-framed display cases of any kind whatsoever; no slate-covered laboratory tables; no high shelves holding mysterious equipment of elongated metal and blown glass; no mortared archways set with mosaic tile and leading to watery chambers below. Here was no move-ment of any kind, whether of students in white coats peering at birds or pouring thin liquids from one flask to another, or of athletes acting out in unison varieties of complex gestures and

exercises telegraphed to them from the dead. Here, in contrast
with those places, was no one; here were no sounds or voices
or movement whatsoever; here, it seemed to me, at long last,
was nothing.

The building (I went more deeply inside) appeared to contain only wooden-floored rooms, these of a modest size, entirely unadorned, their doors left casually standing open. In the
rooms on one side of the small entranceway, to my right, a gray
afternoon shadow had gathered; while in those on the other
side, declining sunlight fell through tall windows across rows
of wooden writing desks, motes of dust suspended visibly in
the undisturbed air.

Sensing that I was alone, I allowed myself to consider at
leisure and with a growing sense of wonder precisely what it
was that I believed myself to have discovered there. And in the
building's striking simplicity, antiquity, and silence, my awareness was nothing less than this: that from above and below, and
from every side, I was surrounded entirely, only, and wholly by
the presence of what had gone before.

In the worn thresholds leading into the faintly echoing
rooms, it seemed to me that in fact what I saw were the missing footsteps of the dead; just as it seemed to me, too, that I
heard their absence in the old wooden floors themselves, in the
sudden creaks and soft groans that were released quietly and
often at some distance away beneath the weight of my own
steps as I moved tentatively from room to room. It seemed to
me, in other words, that I myself now moved among the very
spirit of the dead, and, further, that those dead were present
in every fiber, in each proportion, and in every particle of the
old building: in the unfinished plainness of the wooden front

door seen from inside; in the unadorned emptiness of the vestibule, its dark wainscoting reaching to shoulder height, a row of empty coat hooks residing on one wall over a small wooden table; in the cracked, hundred-year thickness of varnish on the door frames leading into the rooms; in the extreme lowness to the floor of the tall windows, in the capaciousness of their deep window seats, in the uneven rows themselves of worn and scratched writing desks, which, left in the casual disarray of abandonment, bespoke nothing if they did not bespeak an eternal absence.

.

My long search toward absence, then, in leading me to this place, had brought me to the most productive and fruitful of my destinations so far. Seemingly without doubt, I had found in the old humanities hall at last a true and profound muteness. Equally important—as I was to become more fully aware in the intensity of the days and weeks that so swiftly followed—I had also found at last a means of study that could itself remain both motionless and mute.

In the stillness of the old hall, I understood with an imposing finality that my chosen field of study was indeed to be in the voices of the dead: surrounded here by their great absence, immersed within it, I would embark upon a program of study through which I would no longer need content myself only with being conscious of, but instead could actually enter into the profound silence that (suddenly and clearly I understood this) had itself been created by those many supple, varied, and infinitely suggestive dead voices that I sensed, within the empty rooms of the old building, so abundantly to be absent everywhere around me.

•

The strength of what I had discovered became apparent to me very nearly at once. I knew now of course that my study would take place without motion, and this knowledge brought with it the strengthening result that my own journey, unlike that of however dedicated an athlete, could never be ended merely by a terminating of those essential yet vulnerable movements, solitary or on a field among others, with which a scholar of that kind strives endlessly to pass through an invisible doorway toward union with the absent and the dead.

Even more important, my own work would occur also entirely without sound: my studied immersion into the absence around me, that is, would go forward under the impulse and by the very means of a protective, accompanying, equivalent, and concomitant silence: and I knew now that this silence could in turn, by the same token, never be altered or misconstrued; never be limited, taken away, or denied; could never, in a word, be silenced.

It seemed to me, by the time my explorations and conclusions had reached this point, that never before in my life had I seen so deeply into the possibilities of things or so deeply into the hidden and revelatory nature of my own existence among them. I returned to the old hall in the late hours of the following afternoon, as I did also for a considerable number of subsequent afternoons, believing that both the location and the method of my studies had at last been determined once and for all. On one of those occasions, sitting in a wooden chair chosen randomly somewhere near the middle of the room, beams of sunlight falling in through the high windows, I wrote down in my notebook four numbered items, believing them to identify the foundations of truth underlying the course of study that I had chosen to pursue with all my energies, finding myself at certain moments still breathless with anticipation and awe at the enormity, vastness, and depth of my undertaking. I wrote:

Zoë Handke
The College of West Tree
West Tree, Minnesota
September 30, 1959

> 1) There can be no limit to the meaning of that which is unexpressed;
> 2) that which is unspoken cannot be silenced;
> 3) that which is unmoving cannot be stilled;
> 4) that which is absent cannot be taken away.

Notes.

1. As I collected materials for my new program of study, as I continued my visits to the humanities building each afternoon, and as I went forward there with the practical details of my work, I found reawakening in myself the familiar sense once again of being at the center of all things. I could not have known that this might be a phenomenon related to the forthcoming and wholly unanticipated end of what I believed was to be my permanent stay in the old hall.

2. Reminiscent of what I had felt after swimming, the experience once again removed from me entirely any will or desire whatsoever for travel or physical movement of any kind, yet gave me at the same time an intense and vivid awareness of places far removed from my own.

I still believe it to have been an experience heightened in large part by the daily contact I now had with the legions of dead voices that formed the substance of my study. These, existing of course neither in place nor in time, existed therefore in all places at all times and, through the act of my communion with them, arranged themselves as if at the ends of tendril-like and half-perceived radii reaching outward toward infinity and forming lines of contact between me and them, wherever each of them might appear, with the result that, in one far corner of the universe, hung like a silent star, a gossamer thread descending from it to me, there might be

> *How orderly the kitchen'd look by night*

in another,

> *Last summer, in a season of intense heat,*

and, even farther away, in yet other directions entirely, but each connected to me also by yet another frail and outflung and infinitely graceful thread,

> *God hath sent me to sea for pearls,*

or

> *I was never allowed a candle to light me*
> *to bed,*

or, familiar, silently mellifluous, capable of bringing me, even now once again, very nearly to tears,

> *Ours was the marsh country, down by the*
> *river, within, as the river wound, twenty*
> *miles of the sea.*

3. This infinitely organizational phenomenon, suggestive of the universality and associative power of my studies, grew to exert an influence also on my immediate physical surroundings, and on the humanities hall itself, with the result that my visits there soon came to be marked not only by my sense of the building's dignity, plainness, antiquity, poise, and silence, but by a growing awareness also of its centrality.

The hall's ancient brass thumb latch; the hollows worn into its stone steps; the heaviness of the entranceway door; the modest elegance of its high ceilings; the homely creakings of its wooden floors: all of these seemed to me no longer to be parts merely of the building itself, but to be elements as well of a continuum that expanded outward, in a widening circumference of oneness, toward the limits of imagination and memory.

Thus, standing in one of the deserted rooms, a book open in my hands before me, I found that I was aware not only of the warm, sun-filled silence around me; not only of the unkempt rows of the writing desks that I stood among; not only of the capacious sills of the windows, or of the glass panes of the windows themselves, with their clusters of embedded air bubbles, elongated streaks, and various irregularities and imperfections: but that I was aware also of the firm earth outdoors leading away from the flanks of the building, down past the boundary of the campus, across the tree-obscured river below, and then into the low hills of the prairie that extended beyond the distantmost edge of the horizon.

It seemed to me at these times that the wood of the old hall's floors and beams had been drawn from that same surrounding earth, and that its soft, worn brick, standing exposed to the wind and sun on its low and treeless rise, had gained its very pigment and substance from this underlying soil as well, as if the building had not been constructed at all but had risen naturally up out of the ground so that the two now existed seamlessly as part of one another, and so that I, standing in one of its empty rooms, came to be a part of the old building as well, and came therefore to be connected and commingled also, inextricably and immediately and intimately and irreversibly, not only with all that I could see but also, beyond the limit of vision itself, with all that I could not.

.

(This quality of the old building, its seamless, organic, delicately powerful oneness with the far reaches of the world: this very trait, as it happened, was to catalyze for me an unexpected period of uncertainty that was to change for one last and unalterably significant time the nature of my studies.

Because I believed so firmly that I had already completed my search for a perfected field of concentration, I found myself wholly unprepared when I was faced with the sudden intrusion (for that was how I thought of them) of inexplicably divergent and unrelated materials into my carefully defined curriculum—an event that took me through a temporarily alarming disorientation that I hadn't by any means foreseen.

These intrusions presented themselves at first in small numbers, in ones or twos, failing on certain of my earlier afternoons of study to appear at all, but, when they did do so, coming to me with an unvarying quickness, unexpectedness, and immediacy. The first time such a thing took place, I remember, I happened to be standing near a window with a southern exposure, a book open in my hands, concentrating on a voice hidden somewhere behind and above me in the very farthest and invisible corner of the heavens, a slender thread, as usual, descending from it to me,

> O, *thou art fairer than the evening's air*
> *Clad in the beauty of a thousand stars,*

when, unsought and unexpected, another and divergent thread seemed also to be outflung in a long ductile arc, disappearing low over the far horizon—and I found myself suddenly face to face with the piercingly vivid image, unexisting and adrift somewhere in the sea of my lost childhood, of my father carrying the mirror of a dresser up the narrow stairway to my grandmother's attic room.

My discomfiture at this point was brief, and the immediate fear I had was soothed into a false ease when, on the following afternoon, nothing of the kind happened again. On subsequent afternoons, however, when I was studying in my favorite room as usual, I found new threads again being flung outward, at first only one at a time, then two, increasing in number and frequency until I found my concentration torn apart at certain moments by small handfuls of them flying outward, taking me with them and yet at the same time leaving me behind in the empty room of the remote old hall, so that I found myself staring at once not only at the astonishingly immediate image of my father (I stood at the bottom of the narrow stairway, gazing up) carrying a mirror to my grandmother's attic room, but also, simultaneously, looking at my heart-stoppingly young mother (when?) hanging clothes on the lines in our back yard, or watching my grandmother in her bedroom slippers and curlers on her way to the candy and tobacco store, or even seeing my uncle Victor's black car, one summer morning, turning the corner and disappearing quickly, at the far end of our street, a brief flash of sunlight glinting on its window as it passed from sight.

I could, of course, have had no way of knowing that this hemorrhaging of images into my work, this sudden converging upon me of low, arcing threads that now sometimes reversed the direction of their origin and flung themselves toward me from all directions beyond the horizon, were signs (as my deafness was soon to be another, and, after it, my blindness) that my studies at West Tree were still to undergo one last alteration, and that before very much longer I would make my now unthinkable departure altogether from the hall for the humanities.

The transitional period of my violently diverging and converging threads did not continue, altogether, for a span of more than four or five days, and near the end of this time (on the last afternoon before the afternoon of my deafness), I returned to the hall deliberately steeled by my belief that through will and determination I could once more purify and focus my studies. But this renewed effort proved quickly fruitless, and when I concentrated more intensely than before on something invisible and inaudible and high above,

> *Down far in the avenue she could hear a*
> *street organ playing,*

for example, or

> *The snow had somewhat abated; carriages*
> *and tradesmen's wagons were hurrying*
> *soundlessly to and fro in the winter twilight,*

new threads would spring out all the more unpredictably and abundantly, disappearing like cast lines out over the edges of the horizons, or flinging themselves toward me from those same immeasurable distances away: and there, before my very eyes, my aunt Leonora, in her colorful skirt, would once again be in her chicken house on her farm in Alma, Illinois, placing warm white eggs in a woven basket; or my father, in 1939, on the empty highway alone, would be driving his car toward Three Islands; or my grandfather, late one long-ago summer afternoon in Ambrose, wearing his rumpled suit, would be making his way up the tree-shaded hill from the river, a cigar in one hand, and his other hand (for there I was myself; I was there, walking close beside him) pressed against the small of my back, pushing me upward, gently, secretly, faithfully, reliably, kindly, toward home. These images, in fact, the more I struggled against them, grew only the more rapidly not only in abundance but also in duration and repetitiveness, with the result that, for example, on that long penultimate afternoon and on the next one, the harder I tried to study

> *We lived at the top of the last house, and the*
> *wind rushing up the river shook the house*
> *that night, like discharges of a cannon, or*
> *breakings of a sea,*

or

> *I would give you some violets, but they*
> *withered all when my father died,*

or

One time there used to be a field there in
which they used to play every evening with
other people's children,

all the more numerous were the tendrils that reached suddenly
out, or that sprang up from beneath the horizons and curved
across the sky to converge upon me; so that, the new threads
joining the old, and each repeating itself again and again, not
only overlapping the others but often recurring simultaneously
with them, it came rapidly to seem that they made up a vast
kaleidoscope of fragmented moments all around me, or that an
increasingly turbulent and thickening snowfall of images was
actually descending upon me in the stillness of the old hall,
inside the very room where I sat, its warm shafts of lowering
sunlight stretching themselves imperturbably over the wooden
floor. Late on that final afternoon, finding a means of escape
impossible, fearing the loss and end of my studies altogether,
I stopped making any further effort at all, closed my books
and put my head down on the desk before me, hoping only
somehow that these innumerable radiating threads might grow
attenuated, break, and disappear, and allowing myself, for the
moment quite passively and defenselessly, merely to observe
the shifting, slowly wheeling and falling, recurring, silently descending images that continued to plunge toward me and that
stirred and moved and gathered themselves tightly inside my
closed eyes:

> a) my grandfather sat down slowly on the edge
> of his bed and lowered himself, with infinite
> care, back against the pillows

b) the faces of two young children, drowned
long ago in the canal, were eaten away by eels
swimming in the dark water
c) my great-grandfather, as a young boy in
northern Europe, walked along a road in
sunlight, wearing a belted jacket
d) in the square white house by the canal, on a
summer day, the shades in each of the
windows, one by one, were drawn down
e) my grandmother ran through the side lawn
of our house in Three Islands as I looked down
from my window, her bare feet flickering in the
November darkness, her nightgown flying out
behind her
f) my father appeared in the front door in the
evening, in August, wearing a dark blue suit
and carrying his overnight case in one hand,
bringing the news of my grandfather's illness
g) I stepped soon after into the open doorway
of my parents' room, stood there framed and
exposed awkwardly and absurdly before I
withdrew at once to flee in absolute silence,
taking with me, in my eyes, the images of my
mother's wildly outflung hands, the ghostly
whiteness of her body arched upward in her
ecstasy, and my father's buttocks plunging
foolishly (he wore his tie, his white shirt, his
knee-length stockings) between her open thighs
before, mortified and frightened and sworn
inwardly to silence and wishing myself (as I

believe now I was then being wished) out of
existence, I turned and went away
h) (these images, and others, came in behind
my eyelids, recurring, floating, shifting, turning
there in silence)
i) when I was seventeen, the scattered pieces of
my clothing, flung from my closet and dresser,
seeming to float in a quiet shifting of colors
near the ceiling of my room; my mother, with
the kitchen scissors in her hand, crumpled on
the floor in the wreckage of her despair,
incoherent with sobs, trying to cut the leather
of the beaded pink moccasins she had bought
for me earlier
j) I, sitting on my bed (pressed into the corner,
my knees drawn up and locked against my
chest so that I felt I was unable to breathe)
k) nothing happens, nothing ever happens,
nothing ever did happen
l) I, like my grandmother before me, fleeing
from our house in Three Islands
m) the cake my mother made for my eighth
birthday party, impeccably and lovingly done:
its icing the round face of a clock; its hands
pointed exactly at four hours before midnight
n) my

.

It is, of course, entirely possible that I fell asleep in the room,
although I don't remember having done so, nor do I remember
in any conventional sense the experience of my awakening. I

know that at a certain moment, almost simultaneously, I became aware of three things, although, peculiarly, I felt by then as if I had already, however dimly, harbored a perception of each of these for some time, a fuller and more clear awareness rushing upon me only now. When this moment occurred, I realized, from the angle and color of the light, that I had stayed in the building longer than usual; that the intrusive images had disbanded themselves entirely, had dissipated into nothingness, and were gone; and that I now resided in a cavern of absolute and unmitigated silence, that there was not so much as the slightest vestige whatsoever of physical sound anywhere around me.

The lateness of the hour and the purifying absence of my intruding images fell away to the realm of inconsiderable matters in the face of the panic that rose up within me at this sudden recognition of my deafness. The rush of fear that seized me was commanding in its strength, while I was quite the opposite in my inability to do anything other than respond helplessly to it. Afterward (the experience of deafness itself did not last very long), I was to chastize myself for the abject nature of my response and for my failure in any way to allow reason to guide me. By the nature of my studies, after all, I had already acquainted myself with the deficiencies both of movement and sound, had chosen to immerse myself in the absence of both of these things, had in fact embraced a method of scholarship for the very reason that it could be undertaken in the same soundlessness that made up the inaudible and absent material of its own study. By any continuity of logic, then, I should not have responded with fear at the sudden departure of the last vestige of sound from the universe around me. And yet I found myself, when such a disappearance is exactly what took place, plunged helplessly into paralyzing confusion and terror.

The first impression—it was like watching the sea draw back suddenly a great distance from the shore—was one of disbelief sufficiently disorienting as to strike me with the force very nearly of a physical blow, making me incapable of any movement at first other than to squeeze my eyes shut for a breathless and prolonged moment, as if believing somehow that when I opened them once again (which I did), sounds would certainly have returned again to the world around me (which they had not).

Absolutely obvious to me at once was the understanding that what I had taken for silence before was in fact made up of innumerable tiny sounds; and with the small, distant, and oddly separate part of my mind that remained calm and unalarmed (before, my eyes wide in great circles of terror, I fled from the hall), I was aware of myself carefully taking note of the evidence around me that now indeed I was imprisoned in true soundlessness. What had been the measure of silence before was the measure of nothing now. The familiar, comforting sounds of emptiness and absence were utterly gone: no soft creaking of the wooden floor or tired groan from a distant corner, or from a room across the hall. No voice from outside reached me— sound of a kind I would have paid no attention to before, but, in its absence, was aware of now: a student, perhaps, passing by, calling out to another. I heard nothing: not a whisper of any presence inside the still air of the closed room, no movement from the sheltering old building around me, not the faint rustle of my own clothing, the intake and exhalation of my own rapid and increasingly shallow breathing, no sound like the distant roar of the ocean when I cupped my hands loosely over my ears, and none, either, when I pressed my hands fiercely, and then held them there, against the sides of my head. Inside one of the windows (I stared dumbly ahead of me for a moment), a heavy black fly buzzed against a pane, then half-floatingly recoiled, bumping clumsily against the glass again and again, but in utter, limitless, perfect, absolute, empty silence.

The short time taken up by my experience was in no way commensurate with the strength of the fear it evoked in me, leading me at this point to flee from my chair and run out of the room, in my alarm and haste causing my books to slide from the surface of the writing desk I had been sitting in and scatter themselves across the floor. One of the peculiarities of my feelings at this moment was a suddenly heightened self-consciousness, and so great was the strength of my desire not to be seen that, had I been able to do so, I know I gladly would have made myself invisible even as I fled through the shadowy vestibule and out the front door into the last, gold-tinged, declining beams of sunlight that flung themselves in long thin paths across lawns and walkways outdoors. As it happened, the lateness of the hour suited my purposes well, for it was by now the time when dinner was ordinarily served, and few, or none, were there to observe the spectacle I presented as I fled—my face a wide-eyed portrait of terror, my hair flying, my hands pressed insanely against my ears; and my flight, as I think of it in retrospect now, was little more than the likeness of a pebble or mote falling unnoticed into an imperturbable and placid world. Sounds came back to me almost immediately, but one by one, in added layers, returning to me as if in widening concentric circles, from farther and farther away: the abundant, crude, shameless, air-seizing gasps of my own breathing, as if I had just found release from the point of drowning deep underwater; the rapid sound of my own running footsteps, quieting as I slowed my pace; the rustle of drying leaves underfoot on a tree-shaded part of the walkway toward my room; a car passing by slowly, its driver not even turning to take notice of me; three or four students crossing on the far side of the green, coming from one of the dining halls, laughing heedlessly among themselves; the perfunctory barking of a dog somewhere beyond the edge of the campus; the brief, trilling call of a child's voice in a game of some kind; the melancholy, lazy, far-off whistle of a train, drawing nearer, slowly approaching the station in the town.

.

(There remained then only one step in the advancement of my studies and in my immersion into the material of antiquity itself, although I could not yet have known that this step was to take the form of my passage through blindness, nor could I have anticipated the kind or intensity of suffering that might accompany the revelation brought to me in this final moment of my sometimes arduous and often intellectually demanding journey.

A sense of urgency and faint unease pressed upon me now in a way that had not happened before; and, even though I had no idea of precisely what was about to happen to me, and certainly no idea of the finality of its nature, I could not escape the feeling that something of pivotal significance to my studies had begun to occur now in a rapidly progressing way. When I went back to the humanities hall on the afternoon following my deafness, I discovered my books and notebook piled neatly on one corner of the small wooden table that stood (as I have mentioned) under a row of empty coat hooks in the entryway. I was naturally grateful for their recovery, having been concerned that they might be lost, but finding them there inevitably suggested to me also that whoever had found them strewn across the floor of the room, and then had placed them so carefully on the vestibule table, might now have reason to suspect my repeated after-hours presence in the hall and might appear again, perhaps out of curiosity, in the expectation of discovering me there. Intending neither malice nor ingratitude, but believing myself unprepared for a contingency of that kind, I planned accordingly, and when, carrying my books, I entered my customary room on the southwest quadrant of the building, I withdrew into its deepest corner, at farthest remove from the windows occupying two of its sides and as much hidden from view through the open doorway as possible. There, at a wooden writing desk, facing the wall, in the far corner of the room, I took up my studies again and pursued them for the remainder of that afternoon, as I did also for the two afternoons that followed until, at the end of the second of these, my blindness at last arrived to claim me, coming upon me almost but not entirely by surprise, since by that time my newly awakened fear and uneasiness had been pushed gradually toward the outer edges of my awareness as I focused again on my work, the exact nature of which had undergone a subtle and profound change in consequence of my recent immersion into total silence.

For through my deafness, without any doubt, I had been permitted to understand at long last the true nature of silence: that it does indeed hold only nothingness and terror. As a result of this knowledge, I saw now with equal clarity that my search for the meaning of things through their absence was doomed to certain failure unless I were to study first not silence itself, but the myriad small sounds, instead, that make silence possible. It was to these minute sounds, therefore, that I must apply myself with new diligence, knowing (as I knew now) that their near-infinitesimal quietness could not lessen their importance, but that their significance in fact could be made only the greater in proportion to the nearness with which they approached in-audibility, residing closer and then closer still to the unseen veil between them and the surrounding, bottomless ocean of silence itself.

The true object of my study, then, as it had been all along but without my knowing how to reach it, remained that very silence: but silence that could exist only with sound to give it meaning; silence that was an echo of itself in sound.

With these new understandings, then, I returned to the books I had left behind me when I fled, and I began my new attempt, not to plunge directly into the terrible silence that rested in my hands, but to enable myself to hear first the remote whispers, the far-off cadences and rhythms, the quietly purling strings of unmouthed and fragile sounds that brought that silence into being. In method, I devoted myself, in varied sequences and measures of time, to the reading and rereading of a line, a set of lines, a chosen passage, or sometimes an entire work, striving to the limits of exhaustion to recognize and hear all the minutely crafted and whispered sounds each held, however faint and elusive these might be, and however close to disappearing entirely into the nothingness that lay beyond them; of which I knew now that they were indisputably the echoes; and that therefore now drew more closely, at last, to the reach of my perception.

My progress at first, as could easily be expected, was incrementally slow and in few ways visibly dramatic. But gradually, with intensified effort, I found myself able at last not only to hear the countless, near-disappearing sounds whose subtlety and meaning had so effectively eluded me before, but simultaneously and almost invariably to hear also the vast and unwhispered nothingness of which they were at once the echoes, parents, and ancient children, and to which they were now also the tiny doorways. I might, thus, in the old hall, not only become aware, after great effort, of something very like a whispered voice resting silently on the page before me,

> *Whilst thee the shores and sounding Seas*
> *Wash far away,*

and become aware of it also, as before, as existing simultaneously in a high, distant corner of the universe, somewhere behind and above me, a ductile thread once again pendent from it to me; but be aware furthermore of the infinity of silence now so distinctly implied, revealed, and given soundless voice through each of its delicate, all but inaudible, infinitely moving sounds. In this same revelatory way, I might at last become able to perceive the tiny rippling waterfall, suspended in another part of the heavens, hanging there once again like a pale star,

> *As one incapable of her own distress,*

and now also to hear the eternal emptiness moving like a pitiless wind through the frail, tripping innocence of its brief syllables; while elsewhere still, there might be the firmer quietness of

Love, sweetness, goodness, in her person shin'd
So clear, as in no face with more delight,

or the water-flowing and weeping smoothness of

There, on the pendent boughs her coronet
weeds
Clambering to hang, an envious sliver broke,

or, a voice hidden among voices, and yet its presence in the heavens known to me somewhere, visible to my ear,

I wak'd, she fled, and day brought back my
night.

.

(Having come to this point in my studies, I might have believed myself at last at the end of my search. To what extent I genuinely believed that my long journey was over, however, I don't know; nor am I certain—it having been a thing hidden even from myself—to what extent, or with what degree of unease, I may now have secretly awaited the hastening approach of a final, culminating revelation.

Having passed through the earlier experience of my deafness, I wanted to believe that I would be able to meet some unknown but similar event with equanimity and composure. That this didn't prove to be the case, however, was due not only (as before) to the great strength of my instinctive responses, but I believe now that it had to do also with the intricate and unseen plan of the whole, which required that I be impelled toward a window of the hall with a calculated exactness of need that would cause me to thrust it open, but that would immediately afterward flood me with a helplessness sufficient to prevent me from seeking to go anywhere else or do anything further: that would keep me, that is, just there—on my knees, at the window, leaning toward the air outside—long enough for me to absorb fully the precise nature of this last revelation, bringing into existence the long-awaited, ultimate step in the final definition of my studies.

Nor, I must admit, have I ever entirely doubted since that time that there could have existed an unseen plan orchestrated by the informing presence of the dead, or that I may in fact have been guided throughout my journey by those nurturing and cumulative spirits. Consider, for example, that without the seemingly inexplicable incident of my deafness, I would not have fled the old building in terror; would not have left my books behind; and would not therefore have found them the next day, piled neatly in the entranceway. If these things had not happened just in this way, how very much less probable it is that in turn I would have drawn a writing desk into the deepest corner of the room, the more likely not to be seen, or that I would have felt it more reassuring to sit with my back to the windows as I went on with my studies. In turn again, if I had not happened to be positioned just so—in that far corner, my back to the room—it seems to me almost infinitely less probable that, unaware of daylight slipping away behind my back, I would have remained so much longer on that final day than usual, with the result that when my blindness did at last begin to reveal itself to me, its growth corresponded so perfectly with the slow gathering of evening's darkness that for some time I was unaware of the true nature of the terrible thing that was happening to me.

Working in my far corner of the room, deceived by the gradu-

alness (as I have said) with which the progress of my blindness
occurred, I became aware only after an indeterminate time that
the book spread open before me had begun to grow so dim
that, even leaning forward until my forehead hung directly over
its pages, I was almost unable to make out the words I knew
to be printed there. I could remember where each of them had
been placed on the page; I could, for the moment, continue to
hear the quietly purling rhythms of falling syllables with which
they made small doorways into the silence beyond; and I was
able, still, to perceive them hanging distantly, remotely, high in
the wide corners of the heavens. The changing light, however,
and the gradually fading words, caused the question to enter
uneasily into my mind, as it had before but only fleetingly and
obliquely, as to whether, for example,

As one incapable of her own distress

would continue to exist somewhere behind and above me
(there: just there—halfway toward the zenith) even if it were
now, with an elusive and gradual subtlety, to disappear utterly
from the page before me. The question grew more commanding
and urgent, compelling me to ask whether

There is a willow grows askant a brook,
That shows his hoar leaves in the glassy stream

would also cease to be in such a case, or whether

How orderly the kitchen'd look by night

or

There, on the pendent boughs

would also simply disappear entirely, the thread broken, or whether such would be true as well, that

> *I was never allowed a candle to light me*
> *to bed*

would fall away utterly and wholly from existence and out of being, as would

> *Last summer, in a season of intense heat*

or as

> *Ours was the marsh country, down by the*
> *river, within, as the river wound, twenty miles*
> *of the sea*

would fall away, too, into a void, as if it had never so much as been; until something in the particular quality of this rapidly advancing darkness, and something in the pale and now wholly vacant pages before me, caused me to look over my shoulder (for of course I was drawn naturally toward the last vestige of light) across the empty room behind me: where I saw that the tall windows there offered only the same pagelike image of lingering paleness amid a vast, surrounding gloom; and that that pale light, even as I sat watching, was giving way to a silent, turbulent darkening, as if thick black wool were being spun and gathered quickly in the very recesses of the wide, helplessly staring caverns of my eyes themselves.

As happened in the case of my deafness, although it felt considerably more pronounced this second time, I was aware of a remote part of myself that remained calm and observant, like an onlooking voice commenting dispassionately on my actions:

while at the same time, in my other and more immediately be-
leaguered self, I felt, as never before, an absolute terror rising
up within me, and before me, indescribable in the overwhelming surge of its impenetrable depth and massive power.

The result was that for a very brief but intense period, until
I at last reached the window and opened it, I was again separated from myself. Having risen to my feet, I heard the voice
explaining to me that now, with my hands, I was carefully
gathering up my books in order this time, unlike the last, to
carry them with me. The outward composure with which I
seemed to do so, however, closing each of the books in turn
and placing them precisely one atop the other, was belied by
an inward terror so powerful as otherwise to have seized me
wholly: my eyes were in the last stage of a process of blinding
themselves inwardly; my heart, responding to an unheard terror of its own, flung itself with a near-bursting frenzy against
my imprisoning ribs; my body seemed to float uncontrollably
with a sudden, disorienting, unexisting weightlessness. As if I
were capable of seeing or governing myself only through the
voice's description of me, I heard it next explaining calmly that
now I was moving toward the nearest of the tall windows; and,
although I was by this time lost entirely inside the velvet blackness that filled my eyes and therefore also filled the universe, I
saw myself groping my way across the room, bumping clumsily
into one uneven row after another of wooden writing desks,
pushing these aside as necessary to make a path until at last, as
destined from the earliest beginning by the long course of my
studies at West Tree, I reached the window; where, unaware of
purpose or reason or conscious thought, I hooked my fingers
under the curved grips (my books placed already to one side)

and raised up the bottom sash, fell to my knees on the wooden floor, leaned into the deep sill toward the air outdoors, and was conscious for some indeterminate and unmeasurable time thereafter (the voice near this moment abandoned me; I fell back into myself, alone) only of the racking, shuddering, ungovernable convulsions of my body as it leaned there, and only of the astonishing sound of my helpless, wrenching, uneven, jagged, exhausting, gasping sobs, between interminable and depleting chains of which, seizing frantically at the remnants of life itself, I pulled deeply into my lungs, again and again and again, the sweet, warm, soft, autumnal, evening-redolent air that flooded through the open window into the room behind me—air that had come, I felt and at once understood, not only from a thousand miles across the face of the earth, but from the earliest and most distant reaches of antiquity itself, and that now, passing like a soft breath through the window I had opened in the antique old hall, came to sustain, nurture, embrace, and envelope me unendingly, without stint or qualification or falsehood or hesitation or compromise or deceit: moving gently over my arms and hands; stirring lightly through my hair; touching my lips and face and brow; visiting itself upon my sightless, yearning, crying, streaming eyes.

.

(This, then, was what my long journey of discovery had brought me to at last. Through the incremental steps of my difficult, often obscure, and sometimes frightening search, guided throughout by the unseen powers and lingering presences of the college around me, I had come to this ultimate discovery of the circumambient and omnipresent womb of life-giving air itself: in which, I now realized with a perfect and radiant and overwhelming clarity, were contained, eloquent in their absence, all things that had ever become, been, and gone; in which were contained the silent record of all voices that had ever been heard, all words that had ever been spoken, all actions that had ever befallen or been taken; in which, by merit of its own unending life that touches all things and is touched by all things, was contained nothing other than all of antiquity itself, all of time, the accumulation of all moments that had ever been.

.

At that window, through that night, the miracle and breadth of my new understanding revealed themselves to me with a clarity and certainty whose quiet strength grew with the slow diminishment of my earlier terror and alarm. As my unseeing body became gradually more calm, I breathed in more steadily the air that flowed past me through the window, and, in that soft darkness, I understood at last the full dimension of what I had come to perceive, the enormity of the discovery that I had been searching for all along: not only that in this nurturing sweetness, precisely and exactly here, were to be found at once all of life and all of absence; but that here, too, through the hushed and revelatory archives of the air, was to be found at last the final entryway as well for my perfect immersion into that absence. It was this that I perceived in the air: that after my long effort, I had been allowed to become the blinded discoverer at last of a sea in which I could never be destroyed, in whose waters I could never disappear or be drowned; and of course I understood, too, that here at last was the final and ultimate perfection of my studies, the end toward which I had been guided all along: a harmony and balance in which scholar, the medium of study, and the object of study could be one and the same, residing without impediment in a state of unity, durability, mutual intercourse, and oneness. I would become, then, I now understood, a scholar of the air; I would become one with the sweet, eternal, succoring air, as I would with the antiquity, the vastness, the multitudes it contained. Blinded, sitting on the wooden floor of the old humanities building, leaning against the low sill of its open window, my heart calm and slow with the lateness of the lengthening night, I sensed, felt, received the nurturing and storied air. It touched the surface of my skin; it entered my body as I drew it gently into my lungs; it found its way into my flesh; it became dissolved into the secret, living stream of my blood.

.

(At what point my eyesight returned to me, or how gradually it did so, I am not certain. There are gaps in my memory of the night—it is likely, of course, that I slept—although I remember, in the first faint gray of dawn, noticing that once again I could make out the colorless shapes of the writing desks in the room behind me, where I had left them in greater than usual disarray during my passage through them. In the cool air of very early morning I took leave of the humanities building and returned across the quiet lawns to my own room, where from that time on I spent by far the greatest preponderance of my hours and days: at my window, as before, from which I could look back from time to time at the building in whose empty rooms I had passed through so much experience—at that weathered red brick building on its small rise of earth, the wooden clock tower rising above it in unbroken sunlight.

In my room, surrounded by my books and papers, my shoes standing on the hearth behind me as if warming themselves at the memory of a fire, I applied myself with a renewed diligence to my studies, through the medium of the air, of all unseen things and of all things unheard. At my window, in the scent of the breeze flowing lightly over its sill, these things came to me most often like gently moving sounds or lights or colors, emerged into my consciousness at one point or another as if they were faint stars in a vast night sky overhead, then disappeared again, recurrently and endlessly, one after another, like quietly snuffed candles, into darkness. A line of poetry might appear to me, visible and audible at once—there: high and frail, far above—then fade slowly; I would hear the sound, from somewhere, briefly, of splashing water; see the clear and brightly colored image, infinitely far away, of my uncle Victor, lying on the side of a foothill in Wyoming, in sunlight, under breeze-touched pines; or, for a moment from 1948 or 1949, watch my mother and my grandmother, their backs toward me, picking asparagus on a bank of the canal, each of them bent forward at the waist, a chill April breeze tossing their cotton skirts out to one side.

And yet sometimes, most often in the small hours that gathered in the long hollow emptiness after midnight, in the thin, icy, bodiless scent of air that came in at that time through my scarcely opened window, things would reveal themselves to me in a different way, unnerving and frightening me even then with their simultaneity, with their recalcitrant unwillingness to disappear, with their terrible, paralyzing clarity. My dying grandfather sat up on the edge of his bed. My mother, in her nightgown, the flat blackness in her eyes, came silently down the darkened staircase, then into the kitchen. My father stood on the bridge over the canal, his arms on the iron railing, smoke from the cigar in his fingers drifting off. And far away, in West Tree, in my room, waiting there alone amid the poor and shattered ruins of my knowledge, I peered out, unceasingly and steadily, into the enormity of the long and unwhispering night.))))))

EPILOGUE

Themes
Zoë Handke
Huntington 221

1.   The Season

Spring was not early that year, but when it did arrive, it came to stay, bringing with it generous weeks of mild, aromatic, soft-aired days. Foliage returned, at first pale green and frail, then suddenly more robust and abundant. Walkways once again were shaded, buildings pleasantly obscured amid the density of trees.

2.   The Year

My grandfather died on May 11th, a Wednesday, shortly after eight o'clock in the morning. The year in which this event took place was 1960, a date that, when committed to paper, presented itself to me as undramatic and mundane, without mystery, boldness, or strength even in the diminutive march of its numerals left to right from their single strong vertical, past an absurdly tumbling and clownish pair of symmetrical curves, to the staring circle of a wide, unseeing eye, or, perhaps more accurately, a mouth opened in shock or surprise: wordless, dumb, silent, and empty.

3.   How I Learned about My Grandfather's Death

My grandfather's death had been expected for some time, the nature and steady advance of his disease being well known. My preparation for it, as well, had been careful, thorough, and complex. As a result, although at the time I understood with continuing apprehension that greater difficulties awaited me in the future, I was not immediately visited, as such, by overwhelming grief.

At the moment of my grandfather's end, I was sitting in an open-windowed classroom, among other students, writing something in my notebook, or perhaps reaching into my bag, on the floor beside the wooden chair I sat in, to take out a pen or a book. I felt no unusual or revelatory sign or impulse at the moment of the dying; as if it were in itself inconsequential to the alterations that had already taken place in the world around me, I remained unaware of the precise moment of my grandfather's passing out of existence. He had already for some time ceased to exist when I made my way on lightly crowded sidewalks to another building, entered another classroom and took a seat in another wooden chair. At ten o'clock, I walked on a long diagonal across the wide central green to the grass-aproned and tree-flanked building I lived in, went upstairs to my room, and found pinned to my door a folded piece of paper with my name on the outside, and, inside, the message:

"Call home right away"

4.   What I Was Aware Of

I was aware of the crystalline, gentle, sweet air of the astonishingly lovely spring morning; its near-motionless perfection; the remarkable delicacy of the air's aroma, freshness, and warmth; of entryway doors being set open wide and windows raised, the morning air entering into placidly waiting buildings, corridors, and rooms; the softness of the new grass under my feet as I walked toward my building.

5.   Arrangements

I later thought of the activities that followed my grandfather's death as having constituted a brief alteration of space and time, as having made up a ritual and dancelike converging of numbers of people toward and then upon a single point at a single moment, followed by their choreographed dispersal once again outward, as if drawn by invisibly resilient, elastic fibers back to their various starting places. Early in the evening of the Wednesday of my grandfather's death, I boarded a train in West Tree that carried me to Ambrose, traveling through the night. My parents and my brother Julian drove from Three Islands, departing for Ambrose early the next day. Other relatives and friends came from other directions, sometimes from long distances, and of course there were large numbers of people from

Ambrose itself and its immediate environs who would attend the wake, funeral, and reception before the generalized dispersal once again outward in various directions and to points at varying distances away.

6.   The Things That Were Most Memorable to Me

The scent, of course, of the spring air; the slowness of the train on which I traveled, drawing me toward Ambrose in the night through sleeping farmland and small towns, and for a time along the river; the absence, in Ambrose itself, of my grandfather; the pleasantly disorienting strangeness of finding, still there, living in the old town, my uncle Elgar and his wife Alice and their children; the far greater and more disorienting strangeness, as if they had been transported through a veil in time, of seeing my parents there, and my brother Julian; talking in confidence, late at night, with my uncle Elgar, revealing to him alone the nature of my studies at West Tree; the absence of my grandfather in the familiar streets and buildings; the absence of my grandfather everywhere; my mother, at the cemetery, standing as if wholly alone, gazing down silently, lost in the absence of time, into the newly opened grave.

7.   My Return

I returned by train, taken to the station by my uncle Elgar and setting out quite early in the morning. Near the same time, my parents and my brother Julian set out by car on their return trip to Three Islands, with the result that I imagined us for some time traveling abreast of one another in the same general direction, I on the west side of the river and they on the east: my father driving, my mother beside him, my brother Julian in the back seat, reclining crosswise, reading one after another of the comic books he had brought with him. The distance between us lengthened gradually as our paths diverged: the train carrying me up the river but then turning away from it, veering toward the northwest; the road they followed taking them first directly northward but then drawing them around a long northeastward curve and pointing them in the direction of Three Islands. As time passed, the image I had of them grew smaller and smaller as they drew farther and farther away, becoming miniature at first, then a small dot, then the merest speck in some imaginary distant place. Near midday, when I knew they would be reaching Three Islands, the distance was so great that I thought of them not as arriving, but instead as disappearing, winking into nothingness, as falling away beyond some indescribably distant and unseen edge of the world. At that time, when they disappeared altogether, there remained, for me, fully another half of my own long journey northward.

8.   My Observations on the Return Journey

I wept for some considerable portions of the journey, particularly during its first half, although this was a weeping that took place with great quietness, drawing no attention from the few other passengers who rode with me in the car, or from the conductor who passed through from time to time. The train was only very scantily filled during any part of the trip, and it was possible for me to keep a whole seat to myself, leaning my head against the window and looking out at the countryside passing by. The seat across from me remained empty, too, as did the seats in front of me and behind. The windows of the train could be opened by the lowering of their upper panes. My own window had been opened in this way, as had five or six others here and there, and the conductor, furthermore, had left the doors at front and rear standing open, with the result that the fresh air of the warm spring day circulated throughout the car as it moved, creating in it a sweetly scented and softly buoyant loveliness, and filling it also with a seeming weightlessness and light that caused me, with the unremitting loneliness and inconsolably profound isolation I then felt, to imagine that I was traveling in no particular place or time, but instead in any place or time, or even conceivably in none. The train was not rapid; it made frequent stops; and there was a long delay, at the point where we turned away once and for all from the river, when the number of passenger cars was reduced to one, and when this one was connected then to the end of a long line of box cars and tank cars and flatcars made of metal or of old wood and painted variously and in a gaudy assemblage of bright or scarred or almost wholly faded orange or red or silver or black or yellow or brown. This train of many colors drew me away from the river in a long, gentle arc through rolling countryside toward West Tree, noonday sunlight falling steadily across fields in green and varied shades of new growth that led outward to the horizons all around. This train, too, was not rapid, although it stopped far more seldom, its movement steady, continuous, and lulling. The day grew warmer, and the air coming in through the windows and doors became more heavy and somnolent, carrying with it the scent of earth warmed by the sun, and, as we made our way slowly through them, the sweetly nectared aroma of fields of blossoming clover. It seems to me quite likely that I may have slept for some time, as I know the conductor did, in his blue suit, in the rear seat, his head fallen back, the open door beside him allowing a view of the endlessly receding tracks. Alone in the car with the sleeping conductor, I gazed out of my window. Nibbling curls, lapping freshets, passing eddies of soft air moved expressively and intimately about me. On a wide turn, I could see for a time the curved length of the whole train, the engine small in the distance, drawing me still more deeply and farther northward into the continent. Whether asleep or awake, in the quietness, visited by the sustaining air, I know that certain things were gathered together and brought back to me again. I know that I thought of the distant rumble of freight cars in the switching yards across Three Islands in the long-ago nights of my childhood. I saw once again my mother and my aunt Leonora, the train they rode in rounding a wide curve on the summertime plains of southwestern Minnesota, their heads, in unison, moving from side to side slightly with the movement of the carriage. I saw my dead grandfather, in his rumpled suit and stained felt hat, pushing me gently up the hill in Ambrose, on our way home together from the taverns down by the river. And I know I dreamed that my other grandfather, much longer dead, was somewhere just above me: sitting on a kitchen chair on top of the car I rode in, his sleeves rolled up to his elbows, his head thrown back, playing a music on his violin that I could not hear, a music that reached out everywhere, to the distant, disappearing edges of the horizons all around me.

9.   The Termination of My Journey

In the last, declining sunlight of the warm spring evening, I saw the town of West Tree from a window of the train I rode on as it turned to follow a curve in the small prairie river approaching from the south. From a mile or so away, as it came into view, the town revealed itself to me where it lay in gathering shadow on the twin low banks of the river. The college itself, standing on its low rise a short distance beyond the far edge of the town, continued just then to receive the gold-hued flood of sunlight reaching it horizontally from the west. The parts and fragments of its buildings rising up through a green density of spring foliage gave the impression of their being clustered half-ruins, imperturbable remnants of towers and old walls that received, from the light of the dying sun, the steadying glow of antiquity and past time.

When I stepped from the train onto the red-brick platform of the station at West Tree, there was no one else nearby. In the solitude following the train's departure, I walked rapidly into the town, crossed the river, and made my way up the hill, rising as I did so into the now quickly disappearing vestiges of sunlight. Briefly, at the top of the hill, I walked on level open ground; then I entered in once again among the familiar and darkening shadows of trees.

V

NEW YORK

I

My mother, in the end, did not die until late in June of 1975. My older daughter by that time was almost five years old, my younger close to three. We lived—as we had lived for my daughters' entire lives—in our apartment on the West Side, not far from the river.

·

There had been warnings and premonitions of my mother's death, of course, as there had been warnings and premonitions of it—as I had for some time now understood clearly—from the beginning of my life. My mother, more specifically, had attempted to die earlier, before at last succeeding in her long and despairing effort. Ten months after the birth of my first daughter, and then once again a year and a half after the birth of my second, I had rushed suddenly to the airport, flown to the Middle West, and sat beside her where, resting wordlessly and in the long-desired chambers of a profound and visionary sleep, plastic tubes entering her veins and throat, she had lain for uncertain days and nights on the white sheets of hospital beds.

.

Her death was unexpected even so, coming as it did suddenly—although amid weakened health—during a lengthy and deceptive period of seeming equilibrium and resignation and calm. It was surprising as well, not for its having had to do once again with extremely large numbers of green and white pills, but for my mother's decision, in this final, despairingly ecstatic moment, to release her blood at last, at the bathroom sink, leaving for those behind the pitiable horror of its doomed abundance on the whiteness of porcelain and tile.

.

I was then summoned, of course: I was drawn away a last time, as if by a voiceless siren call in my own frightened and responding blood, to the all-embracing and fathomless enormity of my mother's absence.

2

Across the street from our apartment, in one of a row of brownstone houses, a writer lived. I came to know him slightly because he and his wife also had a daughter, near the age of our own first daughter, whom, inexplicably, they had named Atlantis. I met them from time to time on the street, or in the fruit and vegetable shop on the corner, each of us pushing a stroller.

The writer was remarkable for his youthfulness and energy, his unvarying haste, and his earnest cheerfulness. Whenever I observed him he seemed to be smiling, as if he were unable to contain or disguise the inner welling up of some overwhelming good news; even in his gait and in the hurried, loping movement of his body he seemed filled with the joyful confidence of a barely restrained eagerness.

He was writing, he told me, a book about "the world of advertising." For much of one summer I watched him do this.

My second daughter had been born by this time, and when she was still very small, during her first summer, there was a quiet handful of hours each morning when her two-year-old sister attended a miniature school nearby and when the new baby, lying on fresh sheets in her crib, took a long nap. I had placed a desk at one of the front windows of our apartment, and when I sat there in the late mornings, I could look down at the brownstone where the writer lived and see him at work.

Like its four adjoining companions, his building had a small terrace on its top floor facing the street, enclosed by a stone railing, accessible through a widely opened front window. On this terrace the writer slouched down comfortably in a lawn chair he had placed there and wrote on a large pad of yellow paper, his legs stretched out in front of him with his feet resting on the top ledge of the stone railing. Most interesting to me in watching him work was that beside him on the floor of the terrace, where he could reach it effortlessly and without changing his position, was a telephone, its white cord disappearing through the open window into a room inside; and that frequently, as I gazed down and watched him, he received lengthy calls on this telephone. Sometimes he wrote hurriedly on his yellow pad as he took them; at other times he gazed up toward the sky, somewhere near the zenith, and, with the telephone pressed to one ear, repeatedly and often quite rapidly combed his free hand, from front to back, through his hair.

Some time after this—as much as two or three years later—the story I had seen him writing appeared on television. For two of the three nights that it was on the air, Malcolm and I watched it. I felt gloom and sorrow to find that it was a hollow story, and that a deathlike wind of vast emptiness moved silently among its frighteningly vacuous words. On the small screen of the television set, figures gestured, entered and left rooms, cast backward glances, and often were shown being transported from one place to another by car. Young actresses with shoulder-length hair spoke of betrayed love affairs, deceit, and the loss of great fortunes in promised wealth. At some moments they raised their voices in high, dramatic rage; at others, they wept inconsolably. Regularly, they were comforted, and their feelings were assuaged, by imperturbable older men who wore dark suits, frequently clenched their powerful jaws, and possessed uniformly strong chins.

It was curious to me that these were the things that all along had caused the young writer across the street to seem so unflaggingly earnest and optimistic and buoyant; the things that had come to him, morning after morning, through the thin white cord that had twined its way in through the open window; the things that he had received and gathered together slowly from what unknown number of distant and far-flung places, clutching the telephone to his head as he wrote feverishly on his yellow pad, or as he gazed for long periods up into the vaulted sky, looking as if he were at one and the same time spellbound and eagerly impatient, the hidden, lost ghosts of a wide and unfathomable land whispering their ecstatic secrets into his ear.

There was, however, no question of my asking him directly about these matters. A number of months, perhaps close to a year, before I saw his story on television, he and his family moved away from the house across the street, leaving it for some time empty behind them. Never again did I hear of them or see them. It was as if they had never existed; as if they never were; as if they had been swallowed suddenly into the depths of some unnamed and fathomless sea.

3

As in all dreams, much is real, but the unreal is true as well. I am at work, in my small office high in the ornate building that bestrides Park Avenue at Forty-seventh Street. My desk faces the window, and through the glass I can look out unobstructedly for some miles northward, to where the receding sweep of the elegant avenue diminishes to a faraway point half obscured in mist and summer haze. I pick up the telephone on my desk (although it has not rung), and as usual my mother's voice is in it, speaking to me from the interior of the continent, from a thousand miles away, from the telephone on the wall over her impeccably uncluttered kitchen table.

"I'm dying now," she tells me. As always, although I know that everything has happened already, that she is speaking to me from beyond the grave, my body tenses in fear and alarm, my voice becomes urgent and imploring. "Mother," I say, entreating her, "don't call at home. You mustn't call at home. You know I'm not there."

Malcolm is at home at this time, in our apartment on the West Side, taking care of our two daughters. In the afternoon there is a thunderstorm. As lightning flashes, the three of them sit together on the couch in the living room, Malcolm in the middle with an arm around the shoulders of each of the children, while they wait for the noise of the storm to pass.

When I come home from work, Malcolm greets me at the door. "Your mother called," he tells me in an uninflected, matter-of-fact voice. "She died this afternoon. You didn't call back. It's your fault."

.

Of course I did not disclose to my daughters the manner of my mother's death; and when they asked me about it, I did not answer them fully, although even then the things they knew and had perceived shocked me by being far greater and more exact than I could ever have expected or known.

In this knowledge I felt betrayed and compromised and exposed and helpless. A towering new wave of grief and pity, along with confusion and sorrow, rose up within me: I had failed miserably, even in this, having wanted only to shelter and nurture and protect and harbor my daughters.

Far too often, however, when the telephone had rung, and before I could myself take over the call, or when they had picked up the other phone to talk with their grandmother, they had heard, through that tenuous and invisible cord reaching far back into the hidden and remote heart of the continent where I had grown up, the small, ghostly, hideously caressing promises of death in my mother's whispering voice.

.

My mother's death did not end. Beginning far in the stopped past, it grew with a greedy, unerring, crafted, and painstaking slowness; at last occurred; and then continued, still feasting on the dead flesh of time.

.

(*August 1970.*

My mother is behaving badly. Although the rest of us, as usual, make a brave pretense of being unconcerned or unaware, her mood dominates the better part of our three days together.

Often she will not answer when spoken to. On the beach, she reclines on a chaise longue under the shade of our umbrella, wearing dark glasses and a wide-brimmed sun hat. She remains there for long periods of time without moving.

My brother Julian is a year out of college, and he seems to take pleasure in walking casually up to the hotel bar from time to time and bringing back cold drinks. When, on one of these occasions, he asks my mother if he can bring her anything, she makes no answer, pretending to be asleep. From where I am lying on a towel in the sun, however, a small distance directly to the side of my mother, I can see that her eyes are open, and that she is looking at him.

Near the middle of the afternoon, Malcolm and I go for a walk along the edge of the water. We make our way slowly, in part because we have time to fill, in part because I am big-bellied and somewhat clumsy: our first daughter will be born in a month and a half.

On our way back, although we are still some distance away, I pick out my family once again on the uncrowded beach. An hour or so has passed, and the light of the sun has changed slightly. We approach slowly and unnoticed. My mother remains as she was, on her chaise longue under the shadow of the umbrella, seeming not to have moved. In the sunlight nearby, my father sits on the sand with his forearms resting on his raised knees, his back curved, gazing out over the water. Although it takes me some time to spot him among the few other swimmers, I make out Julian, a moderate distance from the shore, just beyond where the waves gather up to form into low, quiet breakers. He is floating on his back, and the swells raise him up gently, then lower him, then raise him up again.

More than ten years have passed since that long-ago moment. In it, nevertheless, as I look back upon it now where it resides in my memory, it seems to me that the members of my family are captured perfectly, each of them placed in keeping with their character—my mother; my father; my brother. If it were somehow to occur again, if the same moment were to be drawn out of the pocket of time to take place again now, there would be changes but also the absence of changes. My mother, of course, would not be there, and the chaise longue under the umbrella would be empty. My father would be gazing out over the sea, although he would now, as if this had happened to him quite suddenly, have the appearance of an old man. My brother Julian, I am quite certain, would be as he was: some distance from the shore, floating with a studiously maintained passivity, rising and falling gently on the waves.

As for myself, I would be returning from my walk along the beach, drawing gradually nearer and nearer to the empty chaise longue in the shadow under the umbrella; except that now my two daughters would be with me, laughing at the small jokes they make between themselves, taking it into their minds from time to time to run wildly out ahead, and then, in the sunlight—but why should I walk toward the umbrella? why shouldn't I follow my daughters instead?—standing together on the wet sand where the water rushes up over their feet, waiting patiently and calmly and confidently for me to come up from behind.)

4

Malcolm and I moved to the city in June of 1970; I knew then that I loved it, as I would continue to love it, for these reasons: because it was close to the sea, and because it was old. In its streets and parks and buildings, removed from the inland regions of emptiness and death, I could live at ease among the stone and brick, the entranceways and paths, the sculpted friezes and carved ornaments of a long history that at least for now continued to exist without first willing its own end.

.

From the front windows of our apartment, if you leaned out and turned your head, you could see a short stretch of the river framed between the facades of buildings leading down toward it on either side of the street. With the incoming tide, the current flowed one way, another with the ebb. Huge, oceangoing ships sometimes passed across the narrow span of this view as I happened to be watching. They would slide by with a wonderful, regal, easeful slowness, their bows disappearing before their sterns drew into sight. They left behind them a slowly quieting tumult on the water.

.

For me, the old city was filled with scent, and air, and life, and brightly cascading light. Encompassed and flanked and surrounded by rivers and harbors, it seemed to me that it had been given birth by the sea.

.

In hot weather, when the windows were flung open wide, the scent of the river, and of the deep-chambered green sea beyond it, came into our rooms, passed through open doors and along narrow hallways, drifted into corners, touched the ceilings and walls and books, curled downward with the silence of dream or memory onto the tousled sheets of the beds where, in the lingering depths of one summer night following another, we slept.

.

We took the children to the beach, and, when we returned, we brought the sea home with us, trailing sand into the house, bringing back the dampness of the sea in the weight of our heavy towels, its salt coming with us in our hair and on our skin.

.

The building we lived in dated from 1926. The rooms of our apartment itself were large, cunningly arranged, although not enormous. They were blessed by plentiful windows that allowed in air and scent and light, although sunshine itself came in only briefly, for short periods of time each day, and to some degree in accordance with the seasons.

Through the front windows, facing north, sunlight came in only during the airy summer months, after the sun had passed the solstice, and then only obliquely, filling the rooms with astonishing light for an hour or two not long after sunrise, when I, and the ghosts of all those who had lived there before me, gathered near the windows in the brightness.

At the back of the house, where adjacent buildings rose higher than ours, sunlight angled down to warm our windowsills and inch across our floors in a short visit each afternoon, fleetingly in the thinner and more narrow light of the cold winter months, but for a robust and lazy hour in the languid afternoons of summer.

.

Of the comfortably worn and half-decrepit old apartment, I believed this: that in the large bathroom, where I bathed my new daughters in the smooth white basin of the sink, were mingled together with the greatest intimacy and eloquence the building's continuing life and its far-reaching antiquity. The room was large enough for the uncrowded luxuries of a chair, a painted wicker table, and a stool. I remember, in it, whiteness and a soft clarity, a comfortably proportioned spaciousness: and a Mediterranean air, cool and shadowy even in the hottest of summer days, having something to do, it must have been, with the open window, and with the light and air that came in (a plant hung at the window) like flowing, leaf-shaded water, spreading out over creamy thicknesses of aged white paint, over the huge claw-footed tub, the stone-tiled floor and half-tiled walls, and over the smooth, softly glowing and deep ceramic whiteness of the ponderous old bathroom sink, in which my daughters, each in her turn, sat in regal, perfectly foolish and happy splendor, slippery-skinned and wet-headed, splashing in cool water that had been gathered a great distance away, drawn from the flanks of wooded mountains; that had been brought through a remarkable intricacy of ancient conduits to the calm, poised, generous, and old-fashioned cool whiteness of this room; and that then, having bathed the small bodies and smooth limbs of my young daughters, would be returned once again to the patiently waiting chambers of the deep and green and light-filled sea.

·

Until this, and except for this: which I cannot hope ever to escape entirely, which filled me with terror and fear for myself and my children, with which at once I knew myself to be inextricably and unwillingly and helplessly complicit and commingled: that my mother, in the unalterable greed and in the despairing, fixed ruthlessness of her wretched and polluting death, altering even memory itself, transformed water everywhere into blood.

·

Her blood, after all, was mine, in the unknowable sea of which I once had struggled. How could I hope now, once again, not to be drawn down beneath its widened and turbulent surface, into its ruined and invisible depths.

5

In the most difficult of the long months following my mother's death, a dream came to me recurrently, sometimes in small fragments or images, sometimes in longer pieces, invariably composing themselves, in one way or another, into the larger dream that continued to return, often waking me in terror.

It was not on its surface complex, and in the manner of all dreams much was left unexplained. I dreamed, however, that for a number of years—it seems to me that it must have been three or four—Malcolm and I and our daughters lived in a wooden seaside hotel in New Jersey. How we came to be there I am not certain, nor how we left. I know that my parents had made a journey to the East in order to be with us, traveling from their home in Illinois. Their presence in the dream was unusual. Rooted firmly in the wide sweep of the midlands, they had not previously lived by the sea.

·

Although I of course made efforts to disguise it from the

children, I was frightened badly in the period following my mother's death; sleep came to me often with great difficulty, often departing from me as well for no apparent reason, stranding me as if alone in the silence of our apartment for uneasy fistfuls of hours in the deep heart of each night. I began to drink, during this period in my life, more freely than I had done before.

Inside the dream, I was frightened in the same way as I was frightened outside of it, and the dream consisted often of my waking up, not into real wakefulness, but into the interior of the dream. Frequently I would hear my voice delivering calmly measured recitations, as if I were at the front of a lecture hall, although I could not see myself speaking, nor were any auditors evident. In darkness, I would hear myself explaining prosaically that it was the large amount of wine I drank that awoke me for a number of hours in the heart of each night. That, and worry about my parents, in particular my mother, who during this visit to the hotel was at last preparing to die.

Our room was at the front of the hotel, facing the sea, a fact for which, in the beginning of the dream each time I dreamt it, I felt overwhelmingly grateful. When I woke up in the darkness, late at night, I would listen to the measured, slow sound of the waves rolling up onto the shore. Beside me in the bed slept Malcolm; nearby, on their two narrow cots, lay our daughters. Sometimes I thought to myself: I will wake up the children and say to them gently, *Listen, there is the sound of the sea.* It was, of course, a lulling, shushing, infinitely comforting sound. A cool night breeze pushed the curtains gently into the room, their gauzy forms palely visible against the faintest of light at the windows. As I lay there in the darkness listening to the sounds of the moving water, I thought often of the places in the world where someday, if there was a future, I would take my daughters. I thought of the blue Mediterranean, of the curving shores of the Aegean, and, for a reason I did not then entirely understand, since I had never been there and knew of it only in imagination, of the coasts of the North Sea.

·

In the mornings, my father did exercises for his heart. Sometimes the children joined him, jumping and prancing lightly in a frolicsome imitation of his movements, and sometimes they did not. It depended largely on my mother's mood, how sullen or angry she seemed, and this, as ever, was unpredictable. Dressed in his swimming trunks, and without a shirt, my father bent numerous times to touch his bare toes, then held his arms horizontally and steadily out in front of him. After this, he reached for the sky and held his arms for some time directly over his head, his face tipped up toward the ceiling. At last, he extended his arms out to his sides and rotated them quickly in stiff, small circles.

From where she sat on the bed, leaning back against the headboard, her legs stretched out before her and crossed at the ankles, my mother watched him. She held a cigarette in one hand, a small glass ashtray in the other. Smoke curled up in a thin blue line from the cigarette. Now and then, moving only one finger, she tapped the ash. She watched my father unflinchingly, with a quiet, patient, knowing scorn, an expression that, from the time of my early childhood, I had seen appear on my mother's face, and had feared.

·

I had no doubt that throughout most of her life my mother had been in pain, and that her pain now was rapidly growing. Nevertheless I mistrusted and feared her. In her recent life she had been happiest, I believed, when my father was near death—himself then in a white hospital bed, emaciated, gasping for breath, his eyes closed, a mask over his face. Had she felt then—watching over my father in his precarious dance with death, when he might at any moment slip away into nothingness—that there were opportunity and purpose in her life? And did she despise him, in the absence of that passionate intimacy, now that, living, he had grown away from his dependence upon her? It was painful for me to observe these things in my mother: such jealousy and rage, her way of loving by feasting on the beckonings and alarms of death. During our years in the hotel, with the pang of such realizations, I began frequently to weep. At night Malcolm awoke in the bed beside me and asked, "Why are you weeping?" He remained mystified and unpersuaded, even after I had explained to him. But then of course he was different from me, he did not love my mother as I did.

.

An aging waiter said to me, "The hotel was built in 1906." He was aloof but kind, erect and slender in his uniform, and he went off with a silver tray balanced on one upraised hand. I stood in the wide lobby holding my children's hands. Together we watched the elevator rise up toward the floors above. It was like a bird cage ascending rapidly through a delicate, filigreed shaft.

.

I dreamed one night that my mother was the future instead of the past. How I knew this I am not certain. She came into the room where I lay awake. Beside me slept Malcolm. Nearby were my daughters, on their cots under the windows where the curtains billowed gently from the breeze off the sea. By this time my mother wore a large pad of white gauze over one eye. She leaned over me and whispered, "I'm going back now. Bring the children. Come and I'll show you the door." In my fear I at once began weeping, her terrifying words sweeping back before me the whole of my childhood, the numberless occasions when she had betrayed and tricked and harmed me, the countless times when, through no will of my own, simply by my existing, I had somehow done wrong. "You're lying," I whispered to my mother through my tears. Then in sudden rage, I said: "How did you get in?" I tried to rise up from the bed, intending to fend off this specter of my mother who, coming from the depraved and hideous emptiness of her grave, had found her way into this room where my daughters were sleeping. But I found myself unable to move, my limbs paralyzed by an unearthly heaviness, as if I were held down under the infinite and unforgiving weight of an impenetrable sea. My mother, in the dream, withdrew from above me slowly, seeming to disappear gradually, without motion; only the round white bandage over her eye stayed imprinted upon my vision, suspended in the darkness of the room above me like a pale moon.

.

I walked with Malcolm one evening along the shore. Darkness fell as we walked, and because I was frightened about the children, I looked back frequently toward the rows of high, lighted windows of the hotel.

"I'm going back," I told Malcolm.

He carried a book in his hand, a finger keeping his place. The smooth waves broke and sent fans of foaming water hissing up onto the beach. The water wet our bare feet and pulled at our legs as it rushed back into the sea.

Malcolm had been drinking wine. So had I. He raised his arm and gestured grandly with his book toward the horizon. "Ah, the sea," he said, "mother of us all." On the horizon rose the moon, a great globe of crimson, its bottom edge sagging downward, distended heavily. Flung across the sea lay a gleaming roadway of blood.

Filled with unnameable dread, I ran across dry sand that was still warm from the sun. In a lighted window of the hotel, my father sat in a bathtub. He scrubbed his back with a long-handled brush.

Standing in the bathroom, I looked down at him and asked, "Where is Mother? What has she done?" Not looking up at me, and speaking in a voice that was matter-of-fact and neutral, he said, "Your mother feels that you have injured her beyond forgiveness. You should not have been born." His penis was erect. Its purple head stood up, taut and swollen, protruding through the surface of the water.

It seemed to me that I ran endlessly through sterile, white, brightly lighted corridors, accompanied only by my own inchoate screams of anguish and terror. But then, unaware of having passed through any door, I was in the quiet darkness of our room; my daughters were asleep on their cots below the windows; the curtains above them, filled by a breeze from the sea, were billowing gently inward. Visible through one of the windows, high up in the night sky, the moon hung round and silent and pale.

.

(I dreamed, again and again, that we were in a far northern part of Europe, on a shore of the North Sea. A pine forest came down almost to the water's edge, leaving only a certain breadth of curving pebble beach. The sea, in the dream, was calm. The air smelled clean and fresh with the scent of the water and with the cool, damp sweetness of the forest.

Always, my daughters were older, though not yet grown. I saw myself walking between them on the pebbles of the shore. I was holding their hands. The older of them was as tall as my shoulder, the younger still more of a child. They were lean and straight and graceful. I saw their backs; all three of the figures were walking away from me.

Invariably, I became filled with anguish and grief, and the distant, keening sound of my own sobbing came to my ears like the rhythmic, steady sound of the waves at night. I was plunged into anguish because I knew that if I could watch those three figures, see them withdrawing gradually from me along the shore, then I myself was not one of them, that I had been taken away: that someone else was walking with my daughters, someone else was touching their hands, feeling the presence of them nearby, hearing the softness of their voices.)

6

I told no one anything, except for Malcolm, or as little as I possibly could. This had been my way throughout, and it remained so, seeking harbor and stability through silence and inwardness and the protracted uncertainty of waiting.

I began to put down, however, in a journal book, a number of memories. These had to do often, as I should not have been surprised to discover, with air and calm and stillness. Sometimes one of these led to another, then to another, and I allowed them to do so. In this manner, I found myself carried gradually backward into the past, sometimes to things that I had seen, sometimes to things that I had seen but forgotten, at other times to things that I had never seen at all. As if through the veils of a silvery and gentle summer mist, I came upon my great-grandmother, sitting in a white dress with parallel rows of small pearl buttons; I saw my grandfather walking one day along a country road into Ambrose; remembered my grandmother in Three Islands, lying on her bed with one shoe on and one shoe off, gazing toward the ceiling of her attic room; and discovered my uncle Victor where he lay, somewhere in the far West, doomed and as if asleep, on a hillside, in sunlight, under breeze-touched pines.

.

In the autumn of 1975 my uncle Elgar and his wife Alice moved for two years from Ambrose to the East Coast, relocating temporarily as a result of my uncle Elgar's work, in which he was then becoming quite successful. Malcolm and I had bought a small used car near that time, in order more easily to take the children into the country, and to the beach. We drove often, on weekends in the summers, for day visits to where Uncle Elgar and Alice were living, forty-five minutes away on the New Jersey side of the Hudson, in a rented house with a swimming pool.

The memories I began to put down, I found, often had to do also with water, and sunlight, and warmth, and nighttime. I slept once more, on peaceful summer nights, in an upstairs room of my aunt Leonora's farm in southern Illinois. I sat again on the front steps of our house in Three Islands, waiting for long summer afternoons to draw to their close. I returned to West Tree: I went in once again among its buildings and its windowed rooms, some of these now gone entirely, and all of them separated and distanced from me, of course, by more than a decade of passing years; by my marriage; by the birth of my daughters; and now, in addition, by the death of my mother.

·

At Uncle Elgar's, we sat in chairs, in warm steady sunlight, around the poolside. We drank bourbon. My uncle Elgar cooked hamburgers on a charcoal grill. Alice made salads, and from the house, on crockery platters, with pieces of ice melting on them, she brought out sliced carrots, and celery hearts, and radishes, and green peppers.

In the blue-tiled pool, my daughters played for hours in the water. Malcolm and I took turns—and sometimes so did my uncle Elgar—staying in the shallow end to teach our younger daughter how to paddle and float. In the second summer, she learned to swim. Her sister, by then, had begun to go off the diving board. I watched her, again and again and again, as she jumped up spread-armed in the sunlight and for the briefest of moments hung suspended—just so, her wet hair flying—high in the air before starting down toward the endlessly inviting blue surface of the water.

·

(Riding home late at night, I often thought of travel to faraway places. Warm night air came in through the open windows of the moving car. In the back seat, our daughters lay sleeping on pillows, exhausted from a day of swimming. Malcolm drove. It seemed to me always that we should keep on going forever. There was a place, just after we crossed the high bridge and then turned down a narrow curving ramp into the city, where for an astonishing moment a view of the great river itself lay spread out before us like an enormous highway: an immeasurably broad and powerful and tide-drawn channel reaching off boldly into an infinite and sea-scented darkness, the stalwartly glimmering lights of the city pressed up to its very edges.

·

(In our apartment, I lie awake in the small hours of the night, Malcolm sleeping on the bed beside me. The weather is warm, the windows are opened wide, the single sheet that was spread over us has fallen twisted to the floor. Around me there is silence, and, in this silence, it seems to me that I am aware of every manner of thing around me. My daughters are sleeping in the next room, near their own open windows, their limbs flung out, their own sheets pressed down toward the feet of their beds, or fallen to the side. Pieces of clothing lie on the floor, to be picked up in the morning, and in the shadowy darkness of the large bathroom across the hall damp towels are flung in a pile over the back of the chair, swimming suits drape the edge of the tub. Our apartment is filled with life, and with air, and with stillness. Far away, out in the kitchen, silverware and knives lie in their drawers, and the dishes we eat from rest in cupboards. Books line shelves in the living room. My daughters' bicycles, one larger than the other, stand in the foyer, leaning on their kickstands, near the closed front door with its chain—we are a family inside, we are sleeping—drawn across the lock.

I do not get up from my bed. I do not fear my wakefulness. I do not fear going back to sleep. I lie there and wait. My daughters are asleep. Malcolm is asleep. All around me, inside the apartment and on the empty street outside, everything is silent with the silence of the night.

I think to myself: *We are here, I am here.*

Through the open windows comes a movement of air, a scarcely perceptible breeze, little more than a stirring of memory and thought. I breathe in the air; and for a time, on my bed, in the night, my family sleeping safely around me, and before I myself sleep, I imagine the looming presence of the continent itself rolling implacably away from us, reaching westward toward its own unmoving heart; and I think also, in the sweetly scented darkness, where it waits in the other direction nearby, of the whispering sea.

.

Beyond that I do not know. The ending, of course, is darkness.

Late one evening some time later, however, when our daughters were in bed, and when Malcolm had fallen asleep over his book in a chair in the living room, I sat down at my desk to discover at least if there might anywhere have been a beginning among the memories that I had gathered. Of this, too, I remain uncertain.

It seemed to me as well, as it had always seemed to me also in the protracted uncertainties of my childhood, that these matters were in great part secrets, to be preserved at all costs in silence. And yet I began to write them; can no longer hope ever to escape having written them; and offer them now to my own daughters, with inexpressible love, and with such hope for release as may lie within what I have written.

I began:

"I am Zoë Handke. I am taller than my mother, although not very much so, perhaps an inch, certainly not more. But I am larger than she was. My bones are heavier, somehow more angular, more squared-off with one another. My flesh is thicker. It seems to me that all my life, in comparison with my slighter and now vanished mother, I have been . . .

September 1981, New York